GRAND THEFT, AUTO

There were five principal structures in a cluster, all tall and warehouselike. KITT motored silently behind one and parallel to another, with Michael and Devon watching for the sentry. They certainly made no secret of their presence. Michael tooted KITT's horn several times and got no response.

"Boy." Michael huffed. "Maybe our guy's cooping somewhere on company time."

KITT stopped dead in the alleyway. *"Michael, I detect that the lock on that building just ahead has been forced,"* said the car.

"Where? Which one?"

"Ten o'clock."

The infrared image of the broken lock dangling from the mangled hasp zoomed up on video screen two and focused.

"Looks like trouble, Devon." Before Devon could reply, Michael was out of the car and running to the storeroom door.

"KITT—pull up," Devon commanded, and the sleek black car followed Michael.

The square of light from Michael's rechargeable flash unit danced on the doorway as he approached. He shoved on the door and it fell inward—definitely broken.

Then he saw Derek Scott, the guard, sprawled on the floor in a pool of his own blood.

GLEN A. LARSON and ROGER HILL

KNIGHT RIDER

#2: TRUST DOESN'T RUST

Based on the Universal Television Series
"KNIGHT RIDER"
Created by Glen A. Larson
Adapted from the episode
"TRUST DOESN'T RUST"
Written by Steven E. de Souza

PINNACLE BOOKS **NEW YORK**

KNIGHT RIDER #2: TRUST DOESN'T RUST

Copyright © 1984 by MCA Publishing, a Division of MCA Inc.

An original Pinnacle Books edition, published for the first time anywhere.

First printing, January 1984

ISBN: 0-523-42181-8

Can. ISBN: 0-523-43169-4

Printed in the United States of America

PINNACLE BOOKS, INC.
1430 Broadway
New York, New York 10018

9 8 7 6 5 4 3 2 1

**FOR
JAMES E. RONDEAU
*who collects 'em all***

TRUST DOESN'T RUST

———————————————————

ABOUT THE AUTHOR

Among ROGER HILL's varied pursuits is the calling of film historian, leading him to the statement that he "was made the same year as John Huston's *The African Queen*." Born in Fort Worth, Texas, and educated at the University of Iowa, Hill has worked as a journalist for major daily newspapers in Las Vegas, Seattle, and Chicago. Since 1977 he has made his home in Studio City, California, and his other interests include music criticism, cartooning, photography, raising Alsatian show dogs and "hunting for decent Chinese food." This is his fifth novel.

1

The place seemed far too much like a haunted house: pitch dark, apparently deserted, and spooky enough to scare the ghost of Edgar Allan Poe.

Two shadows drifted across the face of the sign affixed to the building wall. The sign was comparatively new: red letters on white metal. Red letters usually meant authoritative, intimidating warnings to keep out. Neither of the shadow figures were concerned with the niceties of trespassing. The first shadow flowed across the sign and was gone; the second stopped, blacking out the message. It was shorter, broader, more stunted than the first shadow.

"ON THIS SITE WILL BE ERECTED THE ..." Here the owner of the squat shadow shifted in order to read the rest of the sign aloud: "... THE KNIGHT MUSEUM OF TECHNOLOGY. AUTHORIZED PERSONNEL ONLY. CLEARANCE CARD REQUIRED. ABSOLUTELY NO TRESPASSING." The man spoke in a ragged whiskey growl, reciting the words slowly and with too much caution, like a child afraid of failing an oral grammar examination.

"Get the hell out of the light!" a voice hissed from the darkness past the sign.

The squat figure, silhouetted by the lampposts ringing the outer limits of the compound, continued reading the sign: "KNIGHT INDUSTRIES, INCORPORATED. Humph. Sounds awfully high and mighty if you ask—"

A callused hand in half-cut gloves zipped out of the darkness like a striking snake, yanking the squat man into the shadows by the scruff of the neck.

"Shut up!" said the whisperer. "I told you to keep the hell out of sight!"

"Humph," snorted the shorter man. "You also told me that the infiltration of this ... er, establishment would be simple, friend Anthony. Your exact words were 'a piece of cake.' Considering our somewhat tumbledown descent of that dirt hillock, and our scramble past that damnable barbed wire on the chain-link security fence, I'd say it was more like a scoop of mud pie. Look at us. We're covered from end to end with filth...."

The taller, younger man made a noise of exasperation. Instead of lambasting his companion further he settled on saying, "Don't call me Anthony. That's what my mother used to call me."

"Tony, then." Having capitulated, the squat man rummaged around in the deep pockets of his incredibly filthy and threadbare great-coat and came up with a bottle wrapped in a paper sack. The sack was fuzzy with overuse. The fifth of liquor inside the sack was mostly consumed, but two or three fireball slugs of rotgut remained, and the man decreased their number by two long, soulful swallows. He smacked his lips and stowed the bottle. "Ahh." He looked around, peered again at the sign. "I take it we have arrived?"

"Just like I said," whispered Tony. "Knight Industries." He pursued his lips for a sound-less little whistle of awe—the awe of the dere-lict street person for the chauffeured limousine. Of the two of them, Tony Cox looked more the streetwise young tough, while his squat buddy resembled a mere Skid Row winehead. Tony had always fancied himself a jackpotter. So what if his corduroys were nearly trans-parent. So what that he had exactly two dol-lars and forty-seven cents to his name (stashed in his jacket, since the holes in the pants pockets were too big to serve as a personal bank). So what if his boot leather had a milli-meter to go before breakthrough. Tony Cox was convinced he had what it took to be a winner, and all he needed now was a winning deal to prove his theory. His latest scheme had brought him and his partner on a ten-mile hike through the night drizzle and fog in search of the shutdown Knight Industries facility. Stuffed inside Tony's frayed denim jacket was a folded hank of newspaper he'd scavenged from a Dempster Dumpster full of trash nearly a day ago. The pulpy newsprint was more than simple derelict's insulation— though it did help stave off the chill that had come with the recent rains and fog. Splashed across the center of the front page had been the article that had brought the pair on their latest quest for their latest hoped-for pot of gold. The security lights in the distance, back near the fence they'd jumped a moment before, made little rainbows against the misting fog. If they lucked out with a windfall at the end of these rainbows, it would all be Tony's doing. Winners planned winning plans, he knew. He combed his ragged black hair backward with his fingers, and his cutoff gloves came away damp. He was fairly certain no one had seen them—yet—in the fog and darkness.

"Come on," he whispered.

Together the two men edged along the wall, away from the sign, avoiding the intermittent pools of light thrown into the night by flood-lamps mounted above them on the brick sides of the warehouselike cluster of buildings. High above they spotted windows, but they were secured by thick black bars that ran both vertically and horizontally. A mouse would find passage through them to be a tight squeeze, so Tony scanned around for vents and doors.

"You sure this is the place you want?" came his buddy's voice, from behind him.

Tony blew out a short little puff of disgust. "Quiet, Rev," was all he said, though he was beginning to realize Rev was getting antsy. Probably because the booze was running low. Tony wasn't drinking; his system was high on the adrenaline of anticipation.

He heard Rev pull out his bottle and take another wet slurp of alcohol.

"Put that down and hand me the crowbar."

"Certainly," Rev said, clearing his throat of the cheap muscatel. His voice remained the same ragged growl—as it would always remain. A lifetime of drinking had permanently rawed his throat and voice. "And Moses threw down his staff," he said, stashing away the nearly empty bottle and withdrawing from the flapping folds of his overcoat a medium-sized jimmy bar. "And lo, it didst become a mighty crowbar, that thou mayest break and enter with abandon."

"Shh!"

"Don't shush me, son—I nearly ruptured myself falling down the hill with this thing in my coat." Rev hiccuped and fell silent.

The weight of the crowbar in his grasp bolstered Tony's daring. He peered around a corner and threw his head back sharply, flattening against the wall and plastering his free hand over Rev's mouth. Rev hugged the wall beside him.

Tony leaned close and whispered, "Guard!"

Rev, his mouth still muffled by Tony's hand, nodded vigorously, and in a second the two men saw an oval of light dance around in the open space just beyond the edge of their hiding place.

They froze, like cats tracking a sudden noise.

Tony had no idea how old Rev really was. The old man had to be fifty, at least. His brilliant blue eyes were always rheumy and red-rimmed, and his spudlike Irish nose was laced with broken blood vessels, another product of a lifetime of swilling the sauce. When neither of them could scratch up the price of a bottle, Tony had seen the old dude drink Sterno strained through a loaf of pumpernickel bread. When Sterno was not available, Rev resorted to rubbing alcohol, or filtered shaving lotion. His stomach was either die-cast titanium or an ulcer-ridden disaster area. But what the hell, Tony thought—even *he* had tossed down a shot or two of "squeeze" in his time.

Rev's overcoat was his second skin, and sometimes Tony was amazed by the various things Rev pulled out of it. He often passed Rev items to hold—like the crowbar—and they vanished into the gray folds of tattered tweed, to reappear when needed. Rev utilized his overcoat the way vaudeville magicians once employed their top hats, and Tony wondered whether the old man ever did inventory on the contents. Another thing the coat concealed was Rev's general shape and physique. It went all the way down to his knees. Rev had probably been barrel-chested in his youth, but time, drink, and gravity had all conspired against him. His legs were widely bowed, and he loped along like a bad actor doing a parody of a wild-West gunslinger. Tony rarely took the time to ponder just how he and Rev had become partners-without-contract; they were just *together* one day. Perhaps it was because Rev made such a good packhorse.

"Mmph," Rev said from behind the glove.

"I think he missed us," said Tony, checking.

"A bad sign. Thou shalt not trespass upon thy neighbor and all that—"

"Thou shalt shut up unless you want to get us caught. Don't start that Ten Commandments garbage on me again, Rev; I'm not in the mood." Hefting the crowbar, Tony knelt by the wall and peeked around the corner at ground level. He knew guards looking for intruders expected to see heads at head level, and was therefore concealed for the crucial second it took to check where he could not see.

The courtyard seemed all clear.

"Relax, Rev. Take another slug. It'll make you feel real warm"

"And spiritual, friend Anthony." He eagerly grabbed for his bottle again.

"Yeah. Don't call me—"

"Sorry. Tony, I mean."

Anthony was what Tony had been called as a child, whenever he'd gotten into hot water. Whenever he slipped an extra Snickers bar into his CPO coat and got caught at the candystore, it was *Anthony* who got strapped by his dad, a large, imposing Italian named Amerigo Coscarelli. Whenever Mrs. Coscarelli, his dad's third wife, caught him peeking through the keyholes as his stepsisters undressed, she called him *Anthony* as the belt crossed his backside. And they'd said, "You're not doing the right thing, *Anthony,*" when he'd been expelled from grade school and decided never to return. After he'd run away from home, he began telling those he met in his travels that his last name was Cox. Tony Cox was a nice, anonymous, vaguely American-sounding name. But the few dregs of style remaining in Rev's personality left the old man with the habit of calling people by the most proper form of their Christian name. Thus Rev had to be constantly admonished not to call him . . . that name.

"Y'know, Tony," said Rev. "I don't think we're gonna find anything around here. I mean, when a zillionaire like that Knight guy kicks the—er goes to his heavenly reward, they always clean out the joint, right? Well, what if they—"

"Shh!" Tony snapped. "You think they'd put guards on a place that didn't have nothing in it?"

"Yeah, but . . ." Rev shrugged. "Let me see that writeup again."

"Now?"

"Just for a second."

Grumbling, Tony pulled the folded newspaper from his jacket. If it would keep Rev quiet long enough for him to figure out a way into this place, then maybe it was worth it.

Rev squinted at the headline in the dim light:

INDUSTRALIST/TYCOON WILTON KNIGHT EXPIRES AT
NEVADA ESTATE
Doctors Cite Natural Causes

"Stick close," Tony said as he rounded the corner. Rev straggled behind. Tony walked heel-and-toe to keep his footsteps silent; Rev's shoes were so scuffed and fuzzy it did not matter. They stopped by a rolling steel door secured by a simple padlocked hasp.

"Gimme that," said Tony, grabbing the newspaper and inserting it between the crowbar and the hasp to deaden the noise. He heaved against the bar and nothing happened.

"Jesus!" he exclaimed. "This stuff sure is—"

"Please don't take the Lord's name in vain, Anth—uh, Tony," said Rev.

"Quiet!" With an animal grunt he jumped into the air, bearing down hard on the crowbar. This time the hasp snapped free. They both looked around to see if their noise had attracted any extra notice—it had not—and then Tony held the crowbar up for Rev to see. It was considerably bowed from the strain imposed on it. "Some tools you got us," Tony chided.

"I just took what I could slip out of the railroad switching house before the yard bulls knew I was around," said Rev. "It's not my fault."

"We can ditch it in here, anyway. Come on."

Tony slid the door back and slipped inside. Rev followed, and then the door was closed to a crack.

"Matches," said Tony.

Rev struck a wooden kitchen match against his gnawed and dirty thumbnail. In the feeble glow of yellow light all they could see was stacks of boxes and cartons.

"Storehouse of some kind."

"I don't know about this, Tony. That looks like a lightswitch over there."

"No, don't hit the lights yet—someone might spot it through the door. We wait a second."

"I can't read this article in the dark, Tony."

"Will you clam up! These boxes here are probably full of all kinds of valuable stuff." He laughed to himself. "Guys like that Wilton Knight, guys that rich, why, they even got gold-and-silver plumbing and light fixtures, man. All we gotta do is stay cool and quiet, and we'll case the whole place, a building at a time if we have to, until we find the goods. That article talks a lot about Knight's computer stuff—you know, those new micro-chips and stuff. That junk's worth a lot of dough. All we need is to find some, laying around loose. Then—"

"It's brandy and cigars, my boy," Rev said in the dark.

"You bet. Hand me a match."

"It's too dark in here," said Rev. "Way too dark. As dark as the Stygian depths of Hades, the infernal region to which sinners like you or I might some day venture on our final journey to—"

"Will you knock it off?" Tony said as he tried to read the box labels by matchlight. "Or do you want to go back to the mission?" He chuckled. "I doubt if you ever had a congregation, even." He knew the remark would get Rev's dander up.

"It's true!" Rev protested. "Men of the cloth often fall to strong drink. I fell from grace, that's all. While a holy man I felt proud to call myself the Right Reverend Jeremiah Beaudine. But, as this moniker would advance me little within the company of my newfound friends—the brotherhood of the bottle, gentlemen of the rails, all—I accepted the new name with which they christened me."

"I've heard that story at least eight dozen times by now, Rev. And I still don't believe it."

"An unbeliever. Yet you, too, call me Rev."

Tony shrugged again. "That's because we're partners."

"Just don't call me . . . ah, Jeremiah, okay?"

They both laughed at that, and Tony said, "Sure thing . . . Rev." He dropped his third spent match. "This isn't gonna make it. Hit that light box . . . but make sure the door is shut all the way."

In the dark Tony heard Rev push a power-box switch home. Nothing happened.

Then Rev's voice came again: "I'll strike another match and see if I can find a second switch. I don't think that box is connected to anything. But first . . ." Tony heard the rustling of the paper sack again and knew that Rev was polishing off the bottle.

What he did not expect to hear was the empty bottle shattering on the concrete floor, echoing monstrously in the large, dark room.

"What the hell are you doing!" Tony fought to keep from yelling.

"Sorry, Tony," came Rev's timid reply from near the door. "It slipped."

"Quiet! Wait and see if—"

They both heard footsteps outside the door and froze silent in the complete darkness of the storage room.

The next few seconds were agony for Tony. He heard the rattle of the broken hasp that meant discovery of his deed. Next, the door slid back an inch as it was tested from outside. Then came the glare of the security guard's flashlight probing through the jimmied door. Tony listened for the telltale sound of the guard calling in reinforcements on his FM walkie-talkie unit, but none came.

His eyes strained to see in the darkness. He could feel and smell the cardboard box right in front of him—it was that far from his nose— but was practically blind, lost in the maze of crates and cartons.

Suddenly, the room was awash in blue fluroescent light. Tony's eyes stung and slammed shut in reaction.

"You!" came the guard's voice. "Hands over your head and petrify—just like a statue."

Tony began to raise his hands when he realized the guard could not possibly have seen him. He still had the bowed crowbar in his grasp. Then, from his hiding place, he heard Rev's voice.

"Good evening, sir! I was just passing the evening"—Rev paused to release an obnoxiously loud burp—"in your fine establishment here, out of the . . . .uh, weather, as it were, and I—hic!—ahh . . .." After a beat, he asked in a confused voice, "Pardon me, Officer, but what was it that I was just going to say. . . ?"

Tony grinned. Rev's tone was slurred and stupid, but he was not that lubricated with booze. The old man had reacted instantaneously, picking up a scam to fool the guard into thinking he was just a trespassing wino who did not know any better—and not a thief.

While Rev babbled, Tony began to edge quietly around the crates toward the guard.

His eyes had focused, and he knew where he was now.

Rev tried to continue his spiel but the guard cut him short: "Turn around, hands on the workbench, feet back and spread your legs." The guard's tone was no-nonsense. Tony heard Rev shuffle across the room to his right.

A gray spiderweb wrapped itself around Tony's face as he moved, and he nearly cried out. He hated bugs of all kinds. The warehouse must be full of them. Everything was probably layered in gritty dust and infested with bugs. But bugs could be stomped on, and dust could be whisked away—all worth it, if he could get his hands on any of Wilton Knight's silver-and-gold plumbing fixtures. Greed was a good motivator, and hunger was a better one. It had been two days since he and Rev had eaten, and then the meal had been less than substantial. Tony kidded himself that they were pulling this whole caper to survive. But neither of them had even found the lightswitch, and the guard had gone right to it in the dark. . . .

Tony switched the crowbar to his right hand. Of course the guard had probably had a big dinner and a couple of beers earlier and knew the layout of the joint. Inside these high-tech places *everything* looked like a lightswitch anyway.

Rev was saying, "I have always had the greatest admiration for our young men in uniform. . . ." when Tony rounded a corner in the crate-and-box maze and spotted the security guard.

He was a young, dark-haired guy. Tony's own age. His cap was pushed back on his head and he was dressed in the gray-and-blue livery of Knight Industries security. A .357 Magnum was strapped to his right thigh along with cuffs, mace, and speed loaders for the pistol. No radio.

Tony watched as he patted Rev down. "Just hold still, old buddy," the guard said humorlessly. Tony resented the man. They were the same age, but this guy wore a uniform and was self-important and made his living rousting guys like Rev. And guys like Tony. The guard represented everything that had kept Tony down through the years, eating dirt and doing without.

He raised the crowbar.

In that instant, Tony's irrational hatred for the guard was complete. He despised the authority indicated by the uniform—too much like the police. Knight Industries security was a *secret* police, like the Gestapo, he thought. The guy probably owned a car and ate three full meals a day and had a blond wife with a big chest who probably used to be a high school cheerleader—the type that would never go out with Tony. The guard carried a gun in case he ever had to argue with guys like Tony. The gun was a license to push people around and keep them in the gutter. The guy had even known where the damned lightswitch was! Anything to prove he was better than Tony or Rev. The guy was not human; he had no feelings; he would toss Tony and Rev into the can for life and not lose a minute's sleep over it, oh no—not with that shapely blonde sharing his bed.

Tony walked on the balls of his feet. The guard was four feet away.

In that moment, if anyone had suggested Tony's hatred had achieved a pitch found only in textbooks on psychology, he might have laughed maniacally, proving the thesis. Instead he swung the crooked crowbar and hit the guard just above the left ear, like a tennis pro delivering a smooth backhanded strike. There was a muted *thud* of impact and the guard dropped like a shotgunned bird to pile up on the floor at Tony's feet.

"I thought you'd never get here," mumbled Rev, who turned to regard Tony's unconscious victim. The V of the crowbar had split the flesh just above the man's ear, and the area was dappled in fresh blood. "But now I think a fast exit would be most expedient."

Tony cursed. He hadn't come all this way just so his plan could be scuttled by some idiot guard who happened to stumble in. He kicked the fallen man savagely in the stomach, and a key ring attached to the guard's garrison belt jingled musically.

"Hey!" Rev said. "It's not godly to kick a fallen man, Tony. He's had it. Let's get the hell out of here."

Tony bent to detach the key ring. "Rev, these guys got no radios. They must have half-hour check-ins at a guardhouse or something. I bet we've got at least twenty minutes to scare up something valuable."

"Do you suggest we just start opening boxes?" said Rev, doubtfully eyeing the contents of the storeroom.

"Not when we got us the keys to the golden kingdom." Tony weighed the key collection in his palm thoughtfully. "Remember what that sign outside said about clearance cards? I bet this guy's gone one. It's like a bank card—gets you into all kinds of places. . . ." He rummaged through the guard's flap pockets and in his shirt found an ID card with a coded magnetic stripe across the back. "See?"

"How do you know we didn't trip some kind of silent alarm when we came in?"

Tony was disgusted with Rev's eagerness to leave. "The place would be swarming with cops now if we did, wouldn't it? Don't be such a wimp."

"Tony, I don't think this guy is breathing. . . ." said Rev.

"Don't worry about him. Worry about us. We got the card and the keys and *this*—" He pulled the guard's revolver from its holster and stuffed the extra cartridges and speed loaders into his coat pocket. "Let's lock him up in here and go, and nobody'll get wise."

Tony made for the door but Rev was still staring at the fallen guard.

"Come *on*. Why do I always have to make you catch up with me?"

"Geez, Tony, I think this guy might be dead or something," said Rev, his voice now tiny and sobered.

Now the guard's head formed the center of a small puddle of blood.

"I'm gone," Tony said from the open door. "You coming or not?"

Rev scurried after his partner, switching the inside lights off. The door slid shut and Tony balanced the broken lock in position so that the casual eye would see it as being normal.

The crowbar remained on the workbench where Rev had been frisked. Both men had forgotten it in their haste.

"Which way, which way?" Tony mused, wearing the expression of a kid cut loose in a toy shop. "This way," he decided, pointing. He and Rev kept to the shadows and encountered no additional sentries. Perhaps the man Tony had laid out so neatly was the only foot patrol guard for this particular cluster of buildings. Tony figured the place for minimal security—wasn't it all just a bunch of locked storage houses and defunct laboratories? The property refurbishments that would herald the construction of the proposed Knight Museum of Technology had not yet begun. For now, the place seemed dead. The perfect time for a raid, Tony had thought. And now they had less than half an hour to pull the rabbit that would put them on easy street, just like the infamous cliché. Which building?

They found another imposing sign.

MICROPROCESSOR R & D SECTION. NO ADMITTANCE.

"What's R and D?" said Rev.

"Research and Development. I think this is what we're looking for."

"It says *top-secret*. If this lab isn't operating anymore, why would they leave anything top-secret laying around? It doesn't make sense."

"We'll never know if we don't check, right? See, look—here's the card slot." Tony jammed the guard's ID card into the access and a dot-matrix screen above the slot came to life, spelling out a message in red letters.

CARD INSERTED IMPROPERLY. PLEASE REINSERT.

"Damn machine," muttered Tony, flipping the card over and pushing it back in. By process of elimination and sheer blind luck, he finally managed to get it into the access right-side up.

SCOTT, DEREK JAMES / 0440273202779 / ID
CODE 744-BB
ACCESS CLEARED

The word *cleared* blinked several times and the message blanked while a metal plate the size of a paperback book slid upward next to the access slot.

"What's what?" said Rev.

Tony peered into the boxlike depression. "It's a keyhole." He immediately dug out the key ring, searching for the one that would fit the lock. "The card gets us the keyhole, and the keyhole gets us in." Another thirty seconds of trial and error crept past, with Rev standing lookout, until Tony said, "I think this is the one."

He pushed the key in and twisted. The screen lit up again.

KEYCODE 3826-7773 / CLEARED

"Boy, it's a good thing this isn't the rest room," said Rev. "Too complicated for people in a hurry."

To their immediate right was a knobless metal door set precisely in a metal frame. It slid silently open.

"Bingo!" declared Tony.

"Praise the Lord," said Rev.

"Now let's go help ourselves to Wilton Knight's goodies."

The door slid shut, the screen went dead, and to all outside appearances, nothing was amiss at what had most recently been Knight Industries most important top-secret lab facility.

2

"I'll bite," said Michael Knight, thirty-three thousand feet up in the air.

Professor Devon Miles, seated in one of the broad leather swivel chairs of the Knight 2000 jet, had been peering over the tops of his spectacles at a finely type-set document. He turned his absent-minded professor's gaze on Michael and said, "I beg your pardon?"

The airborne flagship of the late Wilton Knight's financial empire was Nevada-bound in the late-afternoon sunlight. Michael helped himself to a small, neat glass of white wine from the jet's economically compact bar and returned to his seat across from Devon. He admired the gruff British scientist in a way, yet the seriousness with which he took everything had led Michael to bait him for sport nearly constantly since their first meeting.

"I'll go for it," said Michael. "Tell me what FLAG stands for. I'll bet it's not as good as what THRUSH stood for in the old 'Man from U.N.C.L.E.' TV show."

"I never watch television," countered Devon, deadpan. "I wouldn't know."

Devon was tall, impeccably suited, urbane, and proper; Michael was relaxed and jocular. He lounged in his standard personal uniform of jeans, boots, and turtleneck. His black-leather driving jacket was draped across the back of one of the two empty chairs in the main cabin. The sophisticated plastic-surgery techniques of Knight Industries had left him arrogantly handsome in a rough-hewn, whipcord way and he was still getting accustomed to his new face. He found himself seeking out reflective surfaces in which to examine himself.

Devon stowed the papers in his briefcase and removed his glasses as he turned to address Michael, rather like a news anchorman making a particularly lucid point. "I suppose that since your little misadventure in Millston satiated your suicidal need for action, you're entitled to hear the dull part of the responsibility you've accepted."

"Come on, Devon—don't make it sound so dreary. We've been through all that—what Wilton Knight wanted me for and what his plan for me and KITT was. On the one hand, I applaud him. After all, I committed myself to him when he was on his deathbed. But on the other hand, you've got to admit his goals sound a bit strange in shortform. I mean, what he was trying to do, basically, was bring the Lone Ranger into the computer age."

Devon cleared his throat, and for a moment Michael felt as though he was back in high school under the stern gaze of Mr. Keeley, the Principal Who Never Smiled.

"FLAG is an acronym for Foundation for Law and Government," continued Devon. "Our headquarters are just a bit north of Los Angeles, but we have fully equipped branches in Chicago, Washington, D.C. and New York in addition to 'stations,' such as the facility on the actual grounds of the Knight Estate in Nevada. We maintain phalanges such as the ones in London, Tokyo, Sydney, Caracas, and Bonn."

"All that just for the purpose of giving some high-powered, corporate assistance to anybody you judge worthy?" Michael said. "Sounds a little too loose for my taste."

"You neglect to remember the prime motivating factor that drove Wilton Knight for so long, Michael. The thing that so filled him with anger."

"The theft of his designs and patents by corporate criminals like Tanya Walker and her gang back in Millston," clarified Michael.

"With Wilton Knight dead, I am now in full command of the FLAG program."

"Modesty, Devon, modesty." Michael stared

out the oval window of the jet for a moment. "So I'm not the be-all and end-all of FLAG even though I *was* the guinea pig for your biggest field test of KITT?"

"Correct. FLAG has existed as an organization since 1965."

"From the hints you dropped earlier, I'd say it was sort of a combination of the ACLU and Nader's Raiders."

"Astute," said Devon. "But not accurate. I oversaw the administrative concerns from the beginning."

"Earlier, you said it was mostly paperwork."

"Mm, yes. Wilton Knight appointed me personally."

"For your keen organizational mind and your impeccable moral standards, no doubt," said Michael. At Devon's horrified expression he added, "I'm just ribbing you again, Devon." He gave the elder man a second to cool and then said, "So you must have known Wilton Knight while he was working for the OSS during the Second World War."

"How did you know that?"

"Lucky guess. It's true, then?"

"Yes, as you've suspected, Wilton Knight and I go far back beyond our first meeting with you in the middle of the Reno desert."

Michael shifted uncomfortably. "Why don't we just leave that in the past, Devon. Leave Michael Long buried. I'm Michael Knight now."

"After Wilton Knight selected me, I in turn

handpicked a conclave of the country's finest legal minds to staff FLAG's lawyer unit. We accumulated quite a portfolio of technical victories in the courtroom. But one thing Wilton Knight was not prepared for was retaliation."

"You mean appeals?" Michael was frustratingly familiar with the legal loopholes through which criminals often jumped to freedom.

"That, and reprisals. Extra-legal reprisals."

"Oh," said Michael. "You played by the clean rules, but your opponents didn't necessarily feel bound to them?"

"Exactly."

The Knight 2000 hit an air pocket and rumbled briefly. "We're due to land in about ten minutes, gentlemen," the pilot told them over the intercom. "Beginning gradual descent now."

"The people against whom specific FLAG campaigns were targeted did not balk at intimidation, nor did they stop their vendetta actions at mere murder. In the late 1970s, Wilton Knight began implementing his plan to back up FLAG's legal expertise with defensive power that could meet and deal with the criminal mind on its own terms."

"I think this is where I came in," mused Michael.

"Actually, it's where the Knight Industries Two Thousand—KITT—entered the planning stages. Before we selected a driver, we needed an indestructible vehicle in which to put him. Or her."

"But you were racing to complete KITT and make him roadworthy right up to the last minute, Devon. If you had so much time why wasn't the car ready and waiting?"

"We spent the first three years in research, development, refinement, and prototype construction," said Devon. "It took awhile to devise KITT's super-strong alloy skin and develop a chassis that would not crack apart the first time a turbo-boost launched it fifty feet into the air. Plus which, KITT is specifically designed to be modified and updated as our technology improves."

"And a lot of those last-minute modifications had to do with me, right? You told me the seat and instrument panels were customized to my size and reach."

"Well, at six foot four you're a bit over the ideal height for a pilot."

"In the Air Force, they complain if you're too short," said Michael.

Devon waved the protest away. "You're the pilot Wilton Knight chose, based on his own research. I had no part in that."

"So tell me, Devon—are there several versions of KITT loitering around in the labs back at the estate, or is—?"

"KITT is one of a kind," said Devon. "Wilton Knight's first prototype vehicle, the Knight Automated Roving Robot, was not deemed feasible. Somehow the government got wind of that project and wanted to convert the capabilities we'd developed over to defense.

That's when we packed up the California operation and transferred the prototype program to the Knight Estate. Many of the parts developed for the first car were in fact removed and added to KITT. KITT is the only complete model."

"Was the first one the model with the woman's voice?" Michael aid, remembering Devon had mentioned that the programming in KITT was keyed to the personality of the pilot, and that for Michael Knight to drive a car that spoke to him using an electronic amalgam of a woman's voice (as opposed to KITT's refined Boston accent) would be "disastrous."

"Yes, originally—and it's a good example of the sort of gradual modifications I was talking about," said Devon. "When development of KITT's prosthetic voice began, we were confined to using the selective-statement mode of audio taping such as that which was employed in the very first Japanese 'speaking cars' and by the phone company. The vehicle's repertoire was confined to a certain limited library of statements and simple variations on those statements. We actually had a woman from Omaha recite the basic lines for taping. Her name was Agnes, and for a while we thought the car itself was going to be dubbed Agnes, but—"

"But nobody could come up with a suitable set of words to fit the acronym," said Michael.

"At any rate," Devon pressed on, "we eventually developed the male synthetic voice KITT uses now—it's infinitely more flexible, and the micro-processors give it an actual conversational memory. It's not just rote repetition. KITT *thinks*, in his own fashion. His voice sounds human; it has stress and tone and inflection. The first totally mechanical voice we came up with was flat and robotic—very intimidating."

"Like the voice of the computer in that movie where the defense computers subjugate the world?" said Michael, making his own voice a buzzing imitation: *"This-is-the-voice-of-Colossus . . ."*

"I wouldn't know," said Devon. "I never—"

"Yeah, yeah . . . You never go to the movies either, right?"

Devon was a bit flustered.

"Tell me, Devon," Michael went on. "You indicated that the FLAG pilot might have been female. . . ."

"I did?" said Devon, scanning his memory and coming up empty.

"Earlier you said you needed an indestructible vehicle in which to put 'him or her.' Was that woman I saw back at the airstrip—the brunette in the coveralls—was she a scientist or a potential driver?"

"You mean Bonnie?"

"You told me she was KITT's stepmother."

"Oh, yes. Personal mechanic is closer to the mark, Bonnie is one of the Knight Industries crew that helped to develop the improved prosthetic voice, among other things. That semitruck you saw, KITT's roving 'garage,' is her domain. She's purely an electronic mechanic, not an automotive one, although she does understand and can service the functions of the car's engine related directly to the computer."

"She comes with the car?" Michael said, interested. "Tell me about her."

Devon did not know where to begin and had not been expecting the question, concerned as he was with the niceties of explaining the FLAG program. "Well, she grew up in Marin County. Her father was once one of Wilton Knight's private pilots—in fact, it was he who helped her get a position with Knight Industries after she got her degree from Stanford."

"What field?"

"Computer science. She also took a doctorate in robotics. She's very enthusiastic and dedicated."

"But is she—" Michael faltered. "You know. Married? Available? An item with anyone?"

Devon arched one eyebrow. "Is that all you can think about?"

"Hey, don't get the wrong idea, Devon—I just . . . ah, noticed that she's extremely attractive, even in that Knight Industries coverall, and if we're all supposed to be working together . . ." He held up his hands, lamely.

"I think it would be in your best interests to treat Bonnie with a great deal of respect, Michael. Without her, KITT could not have been built, especially not on the tight sched-

ule to which we were all forced to conform.
She's very intelligent as well as being attractive. For someone who has been carping about
my moral sense, I find *yours* lacking in certain areas."

Detecting a distinct tone of paternal pro-
tectiveness, Michael decided not to pursue the
matter. But the brief and tantalizing glimpse
he'd gotten of her at the Millston airstrip remained cemented in his mind's eye. She was
tall, dark, good-looking, competent. He allowed
himself to wonder—privately—whether Devon
was as attracted to his assistant as he was.

The pilot decided to grandstand and circle
the Knight grounds once before moving into
his landing procedure. Michael admired the
view out the groundward-tilted window on
his side of the cabin. Devon packed up his
leather briefcase.

They disembarked together on the far side
of the huge, warehouselike development laboratory where Michael had first encountered
KITT only a few weeks previously. Though
the Knight Estate was devoid of its long-
standing patriarch, Michael noticed a lot of
activity inside the various rooms of the honey-
comblike facility, and in the mansion the
domestic staff was still at work, busily cleaning and rendering everything flawless for his
and Devon's return.

"Once Bonnie returns with the car," Devon
said, continuing their earlier conversation, "I'd

like to field-test a new configuration for the
visual readout on KITT's voice scope."

"The little panel that blinks red whenever
he talks?" said Michael.

"Yes. I think installing a gradated LED readout would be more efficient and easier on the
eyes, don't you?"

They were speaking of the tiny light box
mounted above KITT's steering column. Michael had found the oscillating red light to be
just a little hypnotic. It may or may not have
contributed to his falling asleep at the wheel
shortly before the Millston job. He nodded in
agreement at Devon's description.

"And I think you'd also be able to perceive
KITT's speaking volume visually—in much
the way the LED meters function on the newer
audio tapedecks."

"Oh. I see what you mean."

"There's another piece of field equipment I
need to demonstrate to you, too, later. Something we had no time for when you rushed off
awhile back."

"What is it?" said Michael.

"Have some lunch first," said Devon, somewhat enigmatically. "Sleep for a few hours.
After Bonnie arrives with KITT, we'll work
on the scanners and give the car a general
recharge. Then you and I will depart for Los
Angeles after dark. I'm transferring to the foundation office there to take care of some business. We'll discuss it all in a short while."

Michael could not shake the feeling he had

just been given his orders. "Whatever you say, Devon," he mumbled, mostly to himself.

But Devon had disappeared into the labyrinth of the Knight mansion.

After lunch and a catnap Michael took a crepuscular stroll around the estate grounds. The sun was nosing down behind the mountains to the immediate west, and the sky was the purple of twilight.

He paused against the flagstone wall of an imposing second-story terrace area. It was surrounded by a low stone wall with battlements, like a medieval castle keep. Wilton Knight had liked balancing his teacup on one of the projections and surveying his property from on high, rather like a king.

The old millionaire had blithely given Michael a brand-new life following a horrendously fouled "sting" operation Michael had undertaken on behalf of the Reno police. With a single, deadly gunshot, Police Lieutenant Michael Arthur Long ceased to exist, and in his wake had come Michael Knight. Michael Knight possessed Wilon Knight's name—it was on all of the identification and credit cards provided by the ever-efficient Devon—his immense financial and corporate resources, and even his face. Michael did not know that the plastic surgery that reconstructed his face and changed his fingerprints had been based on World-War-II–era photographs of a much younger Wilton Knight.

But Devon knew. He had supplied the photographs to Dr. Miles, the surgeon.

Michael Knight, then, was a virtual reincarnation of the essence of Wilton Knight—the son and heir he never produced, with the resources of Wilton Knight's entire lifetime, and yet with the youth, strength, quick reflexes, and street smarts that age and disease had finally denied the corporate monarch.

Michael was entitled to a little reality-vertigo. Things and events had been moving at a breakneck pace ever since the sting in Reno.

First the botched police operation, then the agony of recovery from surgery, then Wilton Knight's death, followed by Michael's mad dash to a sleepy computer town called Millston —with a mission to break up the ring of thieves who had stolen from Wilton Knight and nearly deprived Michael of his existence in Reno. Then came Devon and the jet ride back to the Knight Estate. And now, a moment of calm at last, for reflection.

"Michael! There you are." It was Devon's voice.

No moment of calm lasts forever, Michael thought, and turned to meet the scientist, who was halfway through the French doors leading from the mansion to the terrace. He was wearing his lab frock over his businessman's gray three-piece suit.

"Come with me down to the electronics lab. We have a couple of new surprises for you."

His face wore an expression of happiness at some inner, private joke, as though Devon had a child inside his skin who was secretly delighted at such goings-on. Michael saw the expression rarely, and did not yet know Devon that well—he was operating mostly on his instinctive reactions to the man—but he knew that expression meant one or two new scientific toys were in the offing.

"You've arranged it so KITT can change his own tires, right?" It was a pallid attempt at humor. They both knew KITT's special foam-filled tires never went flat.

"More practical, I daresay," said Devon. The two men matched each other's pace as they traversed a scruptulously maintained hallway whose tall ceilings curved into sculpted archways. The floor was polished, gleaming marble and the chandeliers were delicate crystal. Michael felt like he was sneaking away from the tour group at Parliament.

"For one thing," Devon went on, "I think I've come up with an admirable compromise in the matter of your independence."

"*What?*" Michael's defenses went immediately up.

"Oh, purely the negative connotations of the word. I don't mean to curtail your physical freedom. But something the Millston operation made very clear is that when you're on your own in enemy territory, your survival may frequently depend on your ability to contact KITT, and I don't mean by finding the nearest pay phone." Devon nodded curtly to a passing maid who carried a bundle of fresh-cut flowers wrapped up in her arms. "You need a way to contact KITT when you're out of his physical proximity."

"I see." Sometimes Michael wished that Devon would stick to simple English.

"Coincidentally, we overcame the final hurdle in the matter of a compact communications device while we were finalizing the miniature components for the improved vox-box system for the dashboard."

"I think you're bragging, Devon," said Michael. "What do you mean *we* overcame. You mean the Knight Industries technicians overcame—while you and I were flitting about, spending money and having fun."

Devon straightened. "At FLAG we are all one team, thus the editorial 'we,'" he clarified. "But, as I seem to have forgotten, the concept of teamwork is distasteful to you."

"You did say I was the maverick, after all," Michael reminded him.

"Mm." A small expression of hopelessness fleeted across Devon's kind and sturdy features. Michael knew that Devon regularly hobnobbed with the Washington, D.C. gentry and assorted gatherings of people in positions of high power, and wondered how his peculiar approach to wit fared at the average cocktail party. "Apparently the portion of the FLAG effort that Wilton Knight understood better than I," he added.

"Don't worry, Devon—I'm not going to let you down. I just may not always be in touch, that's all."

"This newest development may remedy that," Devon said. "It'll give you continuing access to KITT, and in turn, KITT is usually in contact with us."

"The electronics lab is this way, Devon, not down that hallway." Michael barely suppressed his grin. Devon had been running on, totally ignoring which direction he had been headed toward.

"Oh, yes." The error was immediately forgotten. "As I was saying, as soon as Bonnie returns with the truck and the new vox-box is installed in KITT, we'll depart for Los Angeles. On the way I may get a chance to explain some other functions of the car you had not the time to learn a few days ago."

A man Michael did not recognize greeted them as they entered the lab. Dominating most of one workbench was a grouping of oscilli-scopes and other monitoring devices hooked up to the dashboard light-panel that would replace the one currently inside of KITT. Michael was not prepared for the effect the sight had on him—rather like walking into a room and seeing your best friend's head on a table, smiling and talking to you.

"Hello, Mr. Knight. It's good to see you," said the light-panel, its red, gradated bars jumping, contracting, and expanding with the modulations of the voice. It was not KITT's

familiar Boston twang. This voice was deeper, more gravelly.

Michael realized that the technician was speaking into a microphone wired to the confusion of machinery that terminated in the new vox-box.

"Oh—hi there. So this is what the new indicator looks like." He paused to assess the fluctuating red lines and nodded. "I think you're right, Devon. I like it better." Michael ran an idle finger across the screen.

The technician brought Devon a velvet-lined tray containing several high-tech wristwatches —at least, they looked to Michael like wristwatches, the kind that do a hundred calculator functions and beep out "The Yellow Rose of Texas" when you accidentally press the wrong stud on the side.

Devon removed one of the devices from the tray and said, "We call this instrument the *comlink*." He handed it to Michael.

"I think I heard that term on some old science fiction TV show," said Michael as he tried it on his left wrist. "But then, you don't watch TV, right, Devon?"

"The name is shortform for 'communications linkage'—in this case, linkage to KITT."

"You mean like Dick Tracy's wrist radio?"

"Dick who?"

Michael shook his head. "Right—you don't read the comics, either. I forgot."

The face of the watch looked like any normal liquid-crystal digital watch, albeit with more functions denoted on its tiny display area. Many of the abbreviations and function studs were mysterious to Michael.

"The comlink performs all the functions of any normal digital watch," said Devon. "Time, day, date, stopwatch, alarm, calculator functions, and so on. The red center stud on the right side activates the comlink itself and puts you in direct aural contact with KITT."

"What's its range?"

"It's practical range is two miles. Without obstructions to broadcast, further. And KITT of course has the power to boost your signal if it comes in weak."

"Of course." Michael nodded.

"There are additional functions still in the developmental stage," said Devon. "We're working on incorporating a homing device— two-way, so we can home in on you and so you can track a homing beeper yourself without KITT's help. There's also the video-link— which we haven't quite perfected. Yet."

"This'll do for now," said Michael. "I presume I'm field-testing this, too?"

"Not if he does to that comlink what he did to KITT on this last little excursion," came a voice from the doorway to the lab.

Devon, Michael, and the technician all turned to see Bonnie Barstow with one hand on the doorframe and an irritated expression on her face. She crooked her finger at Devon. "Devon, you and I have to have a little chat about your . . ." She regarded Michael the way she might look at something dead in the roadway. "Your *pilot.*"

Michael's green eyes drank up her image. She was taller than he had speculated on seeing her at the Millston airstrip, where she'd loaded KITT into the back of the Knight Industries service trunk. Close up she seemed even more attractive than what Michael's imagination had conjured up hours before.

He smiled. Winningly, he hoped. "Now Bonnie, wait just a minute—" he began.

He never got a chance to finish.

"*We* haven't been introduced, *Mister* Knight or whatever your real name is. So don't call me Bonnie. Devon?"

"I think she's upset," said Devon, hustling out of the room.

Michael watched them leave, heard them talking heatedly in the corridor. "Observant, that Devon," he said.

The technician standing next to him shrugged exaggeratedly in sympathy.

Michael removed his own wristwatch and strapped on the comlink. It reminded him that KITT was here now, probably sitting outside in the Knight Industries truck. Somehow it reassured him to have his new "partner" in close proximity, even if "he" was not a human being.

"Is there a back way out of here?" he said to the technician. "So I can avoid the flak flying around in the corridor?"

"Sorry. That door's the only way out."

"Well." Michael girded himself. "Once more into the jaws of danger for king and country and all that jazz. Here I go."

"Good luck."

"You, too."

Devon towered over Bonnie but was standing impassively, arms folded, listening as she detailed the catalogue of atrocities Michael realized were adjustments she'd been required to make in KITT due to the rough handling the vehicle had received at Michael's hands in Millston. Devon was in the process of cooling her off with fatherly understanding, professional concern, and deadeye logic. Michael thought that Devon might develop a secondary calling—as psychiatrist to frustrated scientists.

"Bonnie," Devon was saying, "I have to agree with you that Mr. Knight *did* exceed our expectations by actually managing to put a few dents in KITT's hide. But you have to agree with me when I point out that this is exactly the sort of tortuous in-the-field testing that KITT must be able to survive if he is to be of any use whatsoever to the FLAG program. And many of the computer components require periodic maintenance and adjustment anyway—that's part of your job. You—as well as Michael Knight—are not *totally* independent. We are all a team. If, under such circumstances, you find yourself unable to perform, then you're perfectly free to hand in your resignation at any time and—"

The old devil was using the teamwork ethic

as an argument to convince Bonnie, too! Michael marveled at the scientist's sheer diplomatic deviousness.

It worked, too.

"That's not what I was getting at at all, Devon," Bonnie was saying, contrite now. "All right—I flew off the handle a little bit. It's just that I saw the work I had to do, and then had the whole drive back to steam about it."

"Perfectly understandable," said Devon.

"Am I intruding?" Michael said as he caught up with the pair.

Bonnie's eyes flashed as they came up to meet Michael's. Devon smiled a politician's smile. "Of course not, Michael. I've explained to Bonnie the nature of the scrapes you got yourself and KITT into in Millston."

Her expression remained carefully neutral, but she said, "I didn't know you managed to put down the people who stole those secrets from Wilton Knight a couple of years back, Mr. Kni—er Michael. I'm glad you managed that."

Michael decided to play this scene Devon's way. "I'm sorry if I brought back damaged goods. I know KITT's well-being is your business, and I just want you to know in addition that I've grown pretty damned close to that grabby car. I don't want to see him damaged any more than you do." He hoped he'd read her right. She, too, viewed KITT as a person—and not a machine.

"Now that seems much more pleasant," said

Devon. "Michael Knight, I'd like you to meet Bonnie Barstow—and vice versa."

Sheepishly, Michael shook hands with her.

"And with that dreary social duty dispensed," Devon went on, "can we prepare to leave for Los Angeles now? The city council there has convinced me—through a series of costly and earnest phone calls—that our tasks concerning the forthcoming Knight Museum of Technology can wait no longer. We've got to get down to the old lab facilities and storehouses as soon as possible."

"I'm ready now," said Michael. "Let's hit the road."

3

"I believe it was alcoholic spirits that made Noah fall from grace," Rev said. "Or was it Moses? Anyway, I sure wish I had another bottle."

Tony was groping around in the darkness for the lightswitches again. "Never mind that," he said. "Whatever we pull out of here will get us anything we want. And not the cheap paint remover you're used to, either. We're talking blended whiskey, Turkish cigarettes, and wild, wild women; you copy?"

"I don't think there are any commandments specifically against *that*."

Tony's hand chanced across cool painted steel in the gloom. "Ah—here we go."

He engaged a small knife switch and nothing happened. There were at least five medium-sized power boxes set into the wall at eye level, so he grunted dissatisfaction and pushed a second switch up.

There was an electric buzzing, followed by the burning aroma of scorching dust. Tony saw sparks jump inside the box.

"Ouch! I bet none of this crap has been turned on in months!"

Rev struck a match and squinted at the boxes. "Hey, Tony—this one says *danger*."

"Lemme see that. I don't want to fry myself."

A second match was struck, and Tony could see the entire sign.

DANGER / LABORATORY THREE / DO NOT ENGAGE POWER
AUTHORIZED 8/2/82: DEVON MILES

"That doesn't mean anything," Tony said. "Let's go for broke." Promptly he hit all the remaining power boxes. Another one fizzed viciously with sparks, but a worklight on an empty bench across the room came dimly on.

"There," said Tony triumphantly. "See?"

"The Lord moves in mysterious ways," said Rev. "But how come no other lights came on?"

"Maybe they took all the lightbulbs when they moved out. That's the way those super-rich guys are—chintzy when it comes to the basics. At least we can see our way around in here."

By the glow of the single worklamp Tony

could make out a corridor with closed doors
to either side. In crossing the threshold of the
corridor he encountered another unexpected
cobweb.

"Yuch! Damn bugs!" Tony brushed and
slapped furiously at himself.

"Hope all them doors ain't individually
locked," said Rev.

"Why?"

"Because I forgot the crowbar."

"You idiot!"

"Sorry. Had a lot on my mind."

"Yeah, yeah—look, we'll just check the first
door." Tony stepped forward to a door and
twisted the knob. In the hallway it was too
dark for them to read the stencil, which said
LAB ONE.

"No go," said Tony. "She's secure. Let's
look around out here for something to jimmy
the doors with."

They scrounged up a stout length of pipe,
but there was no way to use it as a lever to
pry between the door and jamb. There were
some random pieces of sheet metal—too flexible to be practical. Briefly Tony thought of
using the service revolver he'd stolen from
the unconscious guard, but he wanted to conserve the ammo in case it came down to a
shootout as he and Rev tried to escape. He
decided not to discuss that possibility with
Rev.

Rev, with his unerring nose for locating a
bottle, found some crated glass jugs covered

by a dusty tarpaulin in a corner of the main room. "Looks like the Sparkletts man was here," he said. "Too bad they don't deliver booze."

"Wait a minute," Tony said, pushing past him. He knelt and brushed away the layer of dirt on the crate with the back of his cutoff glove. "Match," he said, extending his hand backward.

By the light of the match Rev produced Tony was able to read the lettering on the side of the crate.

"I think this is the ticket," he said, pulling a bottle out by the neck. It was dusty and tightly stoppered.

"What is it?"

"Acid, man. It'll turn those doorknobs to chewing gum."

"Did you ever think about trying the rest of those keys on the ring you took?" said Rev.

Tony stopped dead. "Oh, God—I completely forgot 'em! Where did I put 'em down?"

"On the table below the power boxes," Rev said, allowing himself to be smug.

"Yeah, right." Tony put the jug of acid down carefully and raced back to the Lab One door with the keyring in his fist. For several seconds Rev listened to him gasp and swear as various keys failed to work. He moved over to the workbench, extracted the crumpled newspaper from his coat, and began to read the article on Wilton Knight's death.

"Hey, did you know this Wilton Knight

guy used to be hooked up with the Defense Department?''

"Damn it! Come on, you piece of garbage!" Tony yelled at the door.

"Not for long, though. He was into every-thing—computers, fuels, chemicals, synthe-tic compounds, micro-processors . . . it says here . . ."

"It bent! The damned thing bent out of shape!"

"Says here no heirs; no family. I guess a buncha lawyers got the whole wad, just like with that Howie Hughes fella."

"Rev! I think this is the one!"

". . . and that he had a big mansion up in Nevada somewheres . . . and probably a whole fleet of limousines . . ."

"Rev! Get over here!"

Rev shambled over just as Tony got the door open. He felt around on the wall for a lightswitch and found none. "Ahh—not again. Look, see if you can move that worklamp over this way so we can see into the room, huh?"

The worklamp was attached to the table by a clamp. By the time Rev got to the edge of the door, the wire on the lamp snapped taut. "This is as far as I can go," he said.

From the darkness inside Tony said, "Hold it up higher so I can see!"

Rev dutifully held up the lamp. He could see tables with built-in sinks, dusty test-tube racks, and a lot of other chemistry-lab glassware. On one table there were two or three corked beakers whose contents had not evaporated. Rev was immediately attracted to these.

"There's stuff all over the floor," said Tony. "They must have pulled out of here in a hurry."

Rev managed to get one more crucial inch out of the lamp cord, making it long enough to allow him to clip the worklamp to the doorframe. The wire hung in the air like a single strand of a huge brown spiderweb. Rev quickly moved toward the table holding the beakers.

"There's nothing in here," said Tony. "I hope the other labs aren't this deserted." They were rapidly running out of time in which to maneuver.

"I wouldn't say that," said Rev, sniffing daintly at a just-opened beaker and then taking a tentative sip of its contents. "Hm. This seems to have lost its bite. Good, though."

Tony moved to the next laboratory door. Rev followed, bringing the beaker with him.

In the main room the power box to Lab Three hissed violently. Purple sparks bounced off the insides of the box, and power was finally established. The box hummed.

The key form was the same for the remaining lab doors, and Tony quickly got Lab Two opened up. Here they found electronic equipment in various stages of assembly. It was all quite alien to Rev.

"We can't hock this junk, Tony," he said.

"Are you kidding?" Tony said. He looked

happier now. "This stuff is just like video games. All you have to know is where to fence it. I can take some of this to Benny the Ritz. He handles this stuff—in the back."

"I don't think you can carry enough to make it worthwhile."

"Rev, some of this stuff has got, like, micro-chips in it!" Didn't Rev understand anything? "They're as good as money, practically."

"I never bought a bottle of port with a micro-chip." Rev sulked.

"Okay, I'll just cut you out, that's all."

"Wait, Tony—if the first lab had nothin' and this one has all this stuff you say is so valuable . . . then what about the other labs?"

"Good idea." Tony nodded. "We'll liberate this stuff if we don't find anything better in the other labs." Enthused, he moved for the third door.

They were deeper in darkness now. The worklamp only extended as far as the door to Lab One.

Rev hurried to catch up with Tony. "Hey, Tony, you was just kidding about cutting me out, weren't ya?"

"Don't worry about it, Rev." The key ring jingled in the dark. "I can't find a key for door number three," he said. "Hey, that rhymes!" He was clearly happier, now that he had found something he considered nego-tiable inside of Lab Two. "Let's try the other doors, then."

Lab Four turned out to be a totally empty

room, and the door between it and Lab Five turned out to be a bathroom. Two more strikes.

"What about that gold-and-silver plumbing?" Rev said, looking at the dusty toilet. The water had evaporated from the bowl.

"Ah, shut up."

Lab Five so discouraged Tony that he made a beeline back to the main room to fetch the acid bottle. He stopped before the still-locked door of Lab Number Three.

"Tony . . ." Rev said uncertainly. "You sure you know what you're doin' with that stuff."

"Nope," he said. "But stand back!"

Gingerly, he unscrewed the locking lid of the bottle and tossed it away down the hall. He dripped some of the thin yellow liquid onto the doorknob, and it instantly began to fizz and smoke.

"That's the way," said Tony.

"Don't inhale the smoke," warned Rev. He would put nearly anything into his mouth, but there was a definite limit to what went up his nose.

The effervescent action died down and Tony gave the door another jolt. The smoke was thicker this time, flowing up toward the ceiling in opaque webs. Something wooden began to burn.

"Think it's ready? We don't have much—"

"Give it time, Rev . . . just give it time."

But Tony was anxious, too, and finally kicked the door hard with his right foot. The lock popped apart and spewed pieces of itself, still smoldering, across the interior of a room much larger than the other labs.

"Hey—there's a staircase in here," Tony said after he poked his head inside. "Come on, and bring the matches."

"I don't like it. It reminds me of a dungeon."

"We gotta leave pretty soon anyhow. Come on already."

Rev followed Tony down the wooden steps in the dark, feeling for the banister and placing his feet down carefully, as though he was blind, or trying to prove to a cop that he could walk a straight line.

"You hear some kind of humming noise?"

"Naw. You're just a little spooked, that's all"

"Shh—I *hear* something. There's a draft down here, too. I think maybe you turned something on back at those power boxes that we don't know about."

"Probably a generator or something. Gimme the matches; we'll take a gander."

Rev's hand was shaking when he pulled the matches from his overcoat pocket, and he let the box slip from his grasp. It bounced once, then vanished between the steps.

"You moron!"

"I still got a loose one left." He handed the single match to Tony, who went out of sight at the foot of the stairs.

The scratch of the igniting match echoed hollowly inside the huge chamber. Rev saw Tony's upraised hand encircled by a corona of fire, a wide concrete ramp leading up to corrugated steel doors at ground level, large monitoring equipment with banks of screens and switches mounted on wheels, and several indistinct but very large shapes, all swathed in heavy tarpaulins.

"Ow! Damn it to hell!" The light went out, and Rev imagined Tony sucking his newly burned fingertips in the darkness below.

In the far corner of the room, Rev saw a red light.

At first he thought it was a vagrant reflection of the match. But the match was snuffed. Afterburn in his eyes, maybe? No—this light didn't dance. It just stayed where it was, pulsating, very intense.

"Tony? You see that?" Now Rev was very definitely spooked. It might be an attack of the DTs, or something even weirder. He did not like it.

"See what?"

Now the tiny crimson light began to track back and forth, like the pendulum on a clock. The humming noise Rev had noticed increased in pitch a few notches.

"Right over there!" Rev pointed—futilely, in the dark. "I think we musta turned on something!"

It was at that moment the taut cord of the worklamp in the corridor gave up, its weight yanking the lamp from its perch on the doorframe to Lab One. The worklamp bounced off the tile floor and its bulb exploded with a loud *pop*. And it became completely dark inside the building.

The abrupt gunshot noise made Rev yelp in terror. He lost his footing and tumbled down the stairs to Tony's approximate location. Junk fell out of his greatcoat all the way down, and then the two bums were alone, clutching at each other in the dark like frightened children.

"Rev? You okay?"

Rev grunted. He'd been thrown out of enough flophouses and inner-city wino bars to know how to fall down without breaking all his bones or getting killed.

The humming noise went up to a louder, turbinelike whine.

"I see it, Rev, I see it!" Tony had fixed on the red light, which tracked patiently left to right and back again. "Let's get the hell out of here! Something's gonna blow up!"

"Amen to that," said Rev, standing. "But which way are the stairs?"

It was Tony who shook off his fear first. "That ramp. Let's run for it!" He grabbed Rev's hand and dragged him in the general direction of the ramp.

The turbine noise hurt their ears now.

"Tony, I think it'd be easier to try to find the stairs," Rev protested, but Tony was not listening.

"What is that thing?" he shouted at the red light. Rev could see the red glow reflecting off Tony's eyes, and nothing else.

There was a keening screech of tires, a sound

both recognized as that of a car jumping from zero to sixty—and the red light grew as it sped right for them.

"Somebody was staking us out!" Tony yelled. "We've had it!" He immediately put up his hands as two blazingly bright headlamps sprang on—one on each side of the red light—and nailed them. Rev was on his knees babbling an incoherent prayer.

The oncoming vehicle did not slow down.

"Hey, okay, we give!" Tony shouted. "You hear me? We give up!"

No dice, he saw.

Tony and the Rev screamed in fear, and then the red light was on top of them.

4

The sleek black form of the Knight Industries Two Thousand—KITT—ate up the highway effortlessly. The vehicle was set into the AUTO CRUISE mode and Michael's hands were off the wheel. The soft glow of KITT's screens and neon readouts lit up the interior of the car vaguely, and from his position in the passenger bucket, Devon considered his own reflection in the window.

"Sorry to get us off so late," he repeated. "The technician took longer installing the new vox-box screen than I had anticipated."

"You mean Bonnie just took more time checking it out once it was installed," said Michael. "KITT, I think she's in love with you."

"But that's impossible, Michael," KITT said,

his new readout screen gauging his words. *"I'm not a human being."*

"A lot of people love their cars," Michael said breezily. "Isn't that ... uh, *auto*-eroticism?" He grinned hugely at his own pun.

"No, you're mistaken. The proper definition is—"

"He's joking, KITT; never mind," Devon said with a grimace.

KITT was silent for a moment, and then added: *"I think his sense of humor does not compute, Mr. Devon."*

"Fine with me," Michael said. "I'd like to keep a few things to myself—and out of my dossier."

"Your dossier is very complete," said KITT. *"Why, in the matter we were just discussing— love—I have in my memory banks the names of all your female acquaintances during the last six months."*

"You're joking now," Michael said, and then caught himself. "No, wait—forget I even said that." By now he knew better than to bring up the subject of KITT's sense of humor— always assuming that a machine could develop one.

"For example," KITT continued, *"beginning with the As, we have Abby, Alea, Alicia, Amy ..."*

"This is not happening," Michael murmured.

". . . Annie, Andrea—"

"Cook it, KITT!"

"Michael, why do you need to socialize with so many women? Wouldn't just one be sufficient?"

"You're starting to sound like my mother. Getting worse than Devon."

Devon grunted, to give Michael the response to his little gibe he required. "KITT is one of a kind. When you're one of a kind, companionship—"

"Does not compute; I'm getting the idea," said Michael, off guard now that KITT had embarrassed him in front of Devon. Abruptly he said, "Is there a dossier like that on all the Knight Industries people?"

"Everyone's in the file," said Devon.

"KITT—what have you got on Bonnie Barstow?" Michael asked with a mischievous grin.

Bonnie's dossier began to roll up on KITT's number-two video screen.

"What do you know?" said Michael. "Birthplace, schools, mother's maiden name . . . height, weight . . . measurements . . . Very interesting."

Devon, annoyed, commanded KITT to cease the playback.

"Let's have Devon's dossier now, KITT."

Devon was not laughing. "I absolutely forbid such a spectacle while I'm present in the car."

Michael chuckled. "I guess I don't need to know *you* measurements, Devon."

"That's another thing I don't understand, Michael," KITT cut in. *"Your obsession with certain anatomical dimensions in the females you—"*

"KITT, can we change the subject, huh?"

"Certainly."

"Actually," said Devon. "If we are to speak strictly, KITT is *not* unique, and that is part of the reason for our sortie to Los Angeles."

"You mean the prototype car you mentioned, the . . . what did you call it?"

"The Knight Automated Roving Robot. Or KARR, if you prefer the shortform."

"Wow. Talk about bad puns . . ."

"I consider my own acronym to be superior," KITT put in.

"Not only that, but somebody beat you to it," said Michael. "KARR is a radio station in Great Falls, Montana. Used to be a gospel station; now they play rock."

Devon cleared his throat, and Michael got the message. "To continue," he said, "the KARR unit was the one the government was so interested in. It had all of KITT's impregnability, but the programming was not as sophisticated."

"They saw it only for its weapons potential?"

"Yes. Most distasteful to Wilton Knight. He politely told them no, that work on the Roving Robot was being discontinued. That was when we isolated and secured our research-and-development facilities on the Knight Estate itself."

"So the KARR is still sitting in L.A.?"

"The unit is in cold storage at the facility we hope to transform into the Knight Museum of Technology. It is one of the things we have to remove before we turn the property over to the city. Preferably we'll dismantle it in the next few days."

"You mean it's still operational?"

"No. It has been totally deactivated."

"How about that, KITT? You seem to have a stepbrother."

"If what Mr. Devon says is true, Michael, your analogy is inaccurate. Such an unmodified prototype would be more like an ancestor in human terms. I would be no more similar to it than you would be to your anthropodial forebears."

"Touché, KITT."

"Nevertheless, it is . . . intriguing to consider . . ."

Michael turned back to Devon. "So our job is to secure the old Knight labs."

"It does seem a bit late for running errands," said KITT. *"Two-thirty-three in the morning. Plus forty-five seconds, to be precise."*

"Blame Devon," said Michael.

"All I want to do is load the prototype into Bonnie's truck after we check in at the lab. We'll take it to the foundation headquarters in Los Angeles and then truck it back to the estate for disassembly. All we have to supervise is the actual removal and loading."

"Perhaps afterward Michael might be disposed toward allowing me a power-pack recharge," said KITT. *"I've not had a full recharge since the beginning of his first mission. That is, our first mission."*

"When one deals with bureaucrats, one gets

accustomed to the wee hours of the morning,"
Devon observed.

"We also have to wait for Bonnie to catch
up with us," Michael said. "Yes?" Hands sitting idly on the wheel (but not guiding the
car), he asked, "I wonder why KARR wasn't
removed before now."

"Because my friend Wilton Knight had the
bad timing to die before he could tie up all
the hanging strings that had resulted in the
production of KITT. And then, of course, we
all had you to deal with."

A tiny LED blinked next to an audio speaker,
and they heard Bonnie's voice fill the car:
"Rook to Knight—say, where *are* you guys,
anyway? You're not anywhere in my sight.
Over."

*"I estimate we are approximately twenty miles
ahead of you, Bonnie,"* KITT replied.

"Better cool it down to about seventy or so
for the remainder of the trip, KITT," Michael
said.

*"But why, Michael—you and Mr. Devon know
of course that there is no possibility of an accident at any speed."*

"What Michael means is that we don't want
to have to wait too long for Bonnie at the
rendezvous," said Devon. To Michael, he
added, "Remember—the computer still tends
to literalize a bit, so you must speak precisely."

"Obliged," said KITT. *"Are you copying all
this, Bonnie? Over."*

"I copy. Don't be such a smart aleck. Over
and out."

                    *   *   *

There was a checkpoint on the access road
leading to the main gate of the old Knight
Industries lab, and a uniformed guard was
awaiting Michael's arrival. KITT rolled quietly abreast of the guard's hut, and the man
inside kicked his feet down from a small drop-
desk and stowed the comic book he had been
reading.

"Michael Knight and Devon Miles, am I
right, gentlemen?" he said, leaning toward
Michael's window. "Pleased to have you here.
I understand you'll be removing some ord-
nance from the old buildings tonight." He ran
his hand along KITT's fender. "Who-ee. This
is the first look I've had at the car. Mighty
pretty."

"Thank you," KITT said. Michael squelched
him.

"Do we just—er, drive on in?" he said.

"No sir," said the guard. "First I have to
run your ID through the monster. Sorry, but
it's standard procedure."

"Sure thing." He handed over his card along
with Devon's, and the guard stepped back
into the hut to check them through the ID
computer. The cards were exactly like the one
Rev and Tony had taken off the unconscious
guard a little less than an hour before.

"This one of your rules, Devon?"

"High security became a priority once we
were compelled to relocate our labs," said
Devon. "Too many people knew things they

weren't supposed to, and they talked, and that frequently got us into trouble. For Knight Industries—its current incarnation, at any rate— this constituttes minimum security. There is this checkpoint, another down at the actual building cluster. The second one houses a sentry who checks periodically on all the buildings. The old labs themselves need card access before keys can be used."

"What happens to this guy when this place becomes a museum?"

The guard was back. "Not to worry. I'm slated to be a museum guard—actually, I'll be guarding stuff more vital than I am now, Mr. Knight."

"Knight Industries tries to avoid paying unemployment benefits whenever possible," Devon said wryly.

"You're both A-OK for entry, gentlemen," said the guard. "At the next hut you'll find a fellow named Derek Scott. He'll help you with whatever you need. Actually, it's about time for him to check in on the phone, so I might give him a buzz and let him know you're on the way down."

The guard hut at the bottom of the winding road was unoccupied.

"Maybe he's patrolling," said Michael. "Let's cruise around and take a look."

Bonnie's ETA is sixteen minutes from now, KITT announced.

There were five principal structures in a

cluster, all tall and warehouselike. KITT motored silently behind one and parallel to another, with Michael and Devon watching for the sentry. They certainly made no secret of their presence. Michael tooted KITT's horn several times and got no response.

"Boy." Michael huffed. "Maybe our guy's cooping somewhere on company time."

KITT stopped dead in the alleyway. *"Michael, I detect that the lock on that building just ahead has been forced,"* said the car.

"Where? Which one?"

"Ten o'clock."

The infrared image of the broken lock dangling from the mangled hasp zoomed up on video screen two and focused.

"Looks like trouble, Devon." Before Devon could reply, Michael was out of the car and running to the storeroom door.

"KITT—pull up," Devon commanded, and the sleek black car followed Michael.

The square of light from Michael's rechargeable flash unit danced on the doorway as he approached. He shoved on the door and it fell inward—definitely broken.

Then he saw Derek Scott, the guard, sprawled on the floor in a pool of his own blood.

"KITT! Devon! He's here! He's hurt!" He knelt to the motionless figure, turned him over, and saw the wide gash where he'd been struck. Devon appeared in the doorway behind them. "Somebody bashed him good,

Devon—and the crowbar they did it with is still here. Look.''

"Good Lord—it's *bent*. Do you suppose they hit him hard enough to—?"

"I don't think so. He's breathing, still. I'm getting pupil dilation. But we need to get this guy to a doctor, and fast!"

"What about the former owners of the crowbar?"

"They've taken off by now. The guard at the gate said Scott hadn't checked in for about an hour. Would *you* hang around?"

"No—but then, I'm not a thug." Devon bent to help Michael heft the prone form.

"KITT!" Michael yelled. "Get in touch with that guard hut! Tell them to get an ambulance out here, pronto!"

"Michael, this man's gun and ID are missing," said Devon.

"Notify the cops, too, KITT. Tell them the assailant is armed and dangerous. So far tonight we've got trespassing, breaking and entering, and assault and battery along with theft of a firearm. Do it."

KITT transmitted the necessary information and then added, *"Michael?"*

"Yeah?"

"I'm registering some unusual power readings."

"From what?"

"Uncertain. As I pointed out earlier, my detection equipment is in need of realignment. I could be picking up bounceback from my own engine,

but I'm also getting what appear to be sensor echoes of my own telemetry."

"What's he talking about, Devon?"

"That's impossible," said Devon. "KITT's equipment isn't that badly misaligned."

"If it's impossible, then ignore it. We've got enough to take care of here."

"I repeat, I'm registering emanations. More strongly, now. To the northwest, at about three o'clock from our current position."

KITT rolled away to investigate.

"Hey, where're you going?" Michael shouted. "Devon, stay with the guard!" KITT was not moving that fact, and Michael ran after him.

Together they rounded the corner that took them to the building into which Rev and Tony had gained entrance by using the guard's keys. KITT stopped.

"Look at the graphs," said KITT. *"Those are not my own readings."* To prove it, KITT shut completely down for five full seconds—and the pulsing indicators on the display graphs to the left of the video screens remained constant.

Michael hurried to the door and inserted his ID card. "Damn!" he said when the access slot slid up. "We don't have the keys."

"Michael, if the suspects are still inside, they still retain the stolen keys. Also the stolen gun."

"Is there any other way in?"

"Affirmative."

Michael jumped into the car with one hand on the edge of the moonroof and the other holding the open driver's side door, riding along running-board style. KITT turned a second corner and stopped in front of the large concrete ramp that tilted downward for thirty feet and terminated in a large door of corrugated steel.

Now the readout graph was really jumping.

Michael started down the ramp toward the closed doors. He wished he'd thought to bring along his set of lock picks, for the first door. Another piece of police hardware that Devon had not yet considered . . .

"Michael, I've registered a sudden boost. I wouldn't recommend—"

The rest was drowned out.

Michael heard custom radials squeal inside the garage bay, and the next thing he knew, the steel door was flying at him in a thousand separate chunks.

Blinded by the glare of headlights, he covered his face and dived frantically to the right. A whirling section of the disintegrating garage door bounced him off the ramp wall, whacking his head against the concrete.

Something huge and black and smothered in dust and debris sped past, just missing turning him to jelly under its wheels.

A hot blast of compressed air and burning fuel knocked Michael down hard. He rolled down the ramp, finally stopping against another piece of the door.

The dirty black shape left the ground and launched itself off the ramp. Instead of pile-driving right into KITT's open door, it cleared the roof of the car by a good ten feet and set down with a crunch eight yards away. Grit flew up from the interloper's rear wheels as it gained traction, picked up speed at an incredible rate, and vanished around the corner with a shriek of tires.

Michael woke up inside an ambulance. A pert, blond paramedic was applying a bandage to his forehead. There were dots of blood on her tunic.

Michael tried to sit up and was slammed down by pain. It felt like someone had driven a cement nail into his skull just above the left eye.

"How's Scott?" he said. "The guard?"

"Guarded condition," said the paramedic. Her badge proclaimed her to be *Hawthorne*. She was pretty and businesslike. "Let's worry about you right now, okay. You tried to field a piece of steel bigger than you and you lost. So hold still for a few more seconds and give the Elmer's glue a chance to set."

"I've always admired women in uniform," he mumbled.

Hawthorne arched her eyebrows, indicating that she heard this sort of rap often.

Michael felt woozy but okay. "Do you always fall in love with your patients?" He got no response, so he said, "Don't worry about my head. I still have a steel plate in there from Vietnam. The indestructible man, that's me."

"I think you're babbling," she said with a patient smile.

"Not about the metal plate."

"How nice, to be able to pick up baseball games inside your own head. So unobtrusive. Okay, I pronounce you more or less fixed. But you have to promise not to do it again."

"Right. Help me up?"

He put his arm around her neck and she hoisted him off the ambulance cot. He steadied himself. His arms were around her neck, and hers were still around his waist.

"Ugh. Got any aspirin for this headache?"

"Sure do." But she made no move to fetch it.

Michael was looking over her shoulder directly into the livid brown eyes of Bonnie Barstow.

"Well," she said stiffly. "I suppose I didn't have to worry about *you* at all." Eyes slitted and mouth turned defensively down, she turned and walked quickly away.

"Pretty lady," said Hawthorne. "You shouldn't let her get away." She disengaged and got him some aspirins.

"I suppose you're right," he said, washing the tablets down with distilled water from a paper cup.

"Michael?" Devon was peering in. His suit was blackened and dusty, and there were smudges on his face. "Bonnie said you were on your feet. What's she angry about?"

"I haven't the slightest idea. What happened to you?"

Devon regarded his ruined clothing. "Shortly after you chased KITT around the corner, there was a horrendous crash. Then there was a car headed for us—at first I thought it was KITT coming back. Then it swerved and tried to finish off both the guard and myself. We barely got out of its path in time."

KITT—" Michael tried to rush for the door and suddenly swayed, hitting the frame.

"Take it easy," Hawthorne said from behind him.

He steadied himself on the doorframe. "Yeah. Is KITT okay?"

Devon looked back over his shoulder. "Right over there," he said.

Bonnie was headed for the black car as well, but when she saw Michael on the trajectory she turned and walked back to the Knight Industries truck.

Michael slumped into the driver's seat. "How ya doing, buddy?"

KITT responded. *"I believe the word you would use is 'rattled.'"*

"No kidding?"

"I don't kid, Michael. Mr. Devon described the KARR prototype to me, but I still don't think I believe it—even after I saw it. That car could have been my twin. It was exactly like

me. It used a turbo-boost to jump over me when it escaped from the garage."

"It's the same model and make as you? Same color and everything?"

"*Identical.*"

"Not precisely identical, KITT." —

In every way I could perceive, it—"

"No," he interrupted. "*That* car tried to kill both me and Devon. Your base programming prevents you from jeopardizing any human life."

The car was silent for a moment. "*I hadn't thought of that.*"

"It was supposed to be deactivated; in cold storage, Devon said. How did it power up? Was there anyone inside of it when it left?"

"*Uncertain,*" said KITT. "*There did not have to be anyone inside, you know.*"

"Couldn't you pick up heat readings from people inside?"

"*As I said, I was somewhat taken aback by the actual appearance of KARR. I did not think to scan him—and if he is shielded as am I, the effort would be fruitless.*"

"Then what you and I both need is a little chat with our pal, Devon," said Michael coldly. "I don't think he's been entirely honest with us about the prototype."

5

Lake Hollywood was as artificial as everything else in the Hollywood section of Los Angeles, but it was surrounded by greenery and its waters were placid and calming. By night the overlook area—a parking verge that gave a splendid view of the lights of the city and could accommodate nearly thirty cars—was a popular make-out hideaway for high school kids.

By dawn, all that remained at the overlook was the accumulated litter and detritus characteristic of the American teenager: beer bottles, crushed aluminum cans, crumpled junk-food bags and empty foam burger boxes. And a single car.

It looked as though some kid had taken his parents' sleek black racer and run it through a dirt-bike track. Grime fogged the windows all around. Thick and impenetrable dust obscured the paint job. It sat alone in the lot of the overlook, its nose two feet away from an overflowing trash drum.

Rev inhaled dust and sneezed violently. A little cloud hung before his nose and then evaporated.

"Wha—!" Tony startled, jerked upright in the passenger seat and banged his head on the window.

A flat, electronic voice said, *"Are you awake?"*

Rev rubbed his rheumy eyes. What he saw did not go away, and a low moan escaped him.

There was no one sitting in the driver's seat of the car, but the dashboard was alive with multicolored graphs and indicators and glowing numerals—none of which had any meaning for Rev. A light-panel on the dashboard blinked in cadence with the voice he heard, but he and Tony were the only two people in the car. As far as either of them could tell, they were the only two people for miles around.

Rev's throat felt caulked up and dry. "Tony ..." he croaked. "I got a *terrible* feeling about alla this. . . ."

"I repeat, are you functional?" said the mechanical voice.

Tony screamed and dived out of the car as fast as possible. He sprawled face-first in the dirt of the parking lot, feet moving to run.

Rev, being in the backseat, had a harder time getting out. He could not figure out how to make the seat button work. "Tony, help!" he wailed, arms waving.

"Who is that?" Tony said, feigning toughness, looking around for the owner of the voice. He remembered his stolen pistol, and hauled it out of his coat.

"Tony, I don't see nobody," Rev said uncertainly.

Tony brandished the pistol. He didn't look very menacing, but he was ready to start blasting until he, too, realized that he and Rev were the only two people around.

"Do you require some form of repair? Are you incapacitated?" the mystery voice said again.

Logic worked its way into Rev's dim and murky consciousness. "Uhh . . . Tony? I think it's the car talking."

The barrel of the gun dropped. "What?"

"Yeah. It's some kinda radio . . . or something." He shrugged and pointed at the dashboard, saying, "It blinks," as though that was an explanation.

Tony scratched his temple with the barrel of the gun. Dandruff flaked away and drifted down. "Terrific," he said. "It's probably the cops, after us."

"I dunno. It asked if we were okay."

"Yeah, we're okay," Tony said, overloudly, to no one in particular. "Except, I don't know where the hell we are."

Both men jumped when the car responded,

addressing them again: *"You are where your companion—currently installed in the back seat— ordered me to stop exactly five-point-two hours ago."*

"Where *I* ordered you to stop?" said Rev, unbelievingly.

"Most of your articulations were incoherent. I do, however, record having heard the distinct word, stop."

"But who are you?" Tony said, to the car in general. "I mean, where are you? I mean . . ." He gave up.

"I am not, as you have speculated, a radio transmission."

Now Rev was visibly nervous. "You're— you're just a car. Ain't you?" He still could not figure his way out of the backseat.

"Not 'just a car.' More properly, I am KARR— the Knight Automated Roving Robot. I am the prototype of the automobile of the future." The voice remained flat and tinny, totally devoid of inflection. Tony and Rev had no way of knowing that the lines they had just heard the car emit were part of the presentational spiel originally programmed into its speech locus for purposes of its unveiling. To KARR's micro-processors there was no time lag between the last time it had been turned off and last night, when Tony inadvertently reactivated it.

"Lord have mercy on us all," Rev said. "You mean you're—you're—" He groped for words and found none to adequately encompass what he was trying to ask. "You're a regular real thing? Not that—that monster you was last night?"

"Yeah," Tony piped in, still waving the gun around idly. "You looked like some kinda red-eyed killer tank or something . . . last night."

Rev turned to his partner. "So how's come you jumped inside of this thing, if you was so afraid?"

"Huh? I don't remember that. All I remember is that it didn't run us down. I saw an open door and I grabbed it. I noticed you was right behind me."

"I was in first," Rev said.

Tony moved around to the front of the car to have another look at the oscillating red sensor light in the hood, but he tarried by the overflowing trash can. He decided to rummage through it and began distributing its contents in a sloppy circle all around him while he scrounged for stuff of interest or value.

"Great," said Rev. "So now we're car thieves."

"This thing's got no license plates, neither," Tony said, leaning over to check. "Cops'll pick us up in a second if we drive it anywhere."
He pulled a grimy, discarded bandanna from the rubbish. It had a railroad engineer's design on it. After a moment of consideration, he tied the scarf around his neck.

"Needs a car wash, too," said Rev. "Hey, you—KARR. How'd you get down in that building, anyway? Who turned you on. I see you ain't got no keys." He looked between the bucket seats. "No keyhole, neither, for that matter. How do you run?"

"Laboratory power was engaged and my awareness returned. The edifice in which you encountered me was the developmental facility in which I was constructed and originally activated. It is also where I was deactivated."

"I told you you shouldn't've messed with those power boxes!" said Rev. "See what you did!"

"Ahh, pipe down. He got us out of a scrape, didn't he?" From the litter can Tony held up a green bottle that had a good three slugs of Ripple left in it. He tossed it to Rev. Rev caught the bottle and chugged greedily from it.

"I do not understand your reference to keys," said KARR. *"I employ none."*

"Forget it," said Rev.

"You are the ones who reengaged my power?"

"Don't look at me," he said, taking another swig. "That was all Tony's fault."

"Thanks a lot." Tony sneered from the front of the car. He was squatting down to look at the sensor now, rubbing dust from its grille with his thumb and watching the pulsing red light.

"I scan you, Mr. Tony," said the car. *"I am indebted to you for turning me back on."*

"Hey, wait a minute," cried Rev, sensing he needed to grab some credit from a potential benefactor after all. "I helped!"

"Then I am indebted to both of you."

"You got it. You can't count on nobody, except for me and good old Tony," he said expansively.

"I will enter that information in my data banks. How may I serve you as recompense?"

"Huh?"

Tony stood up and slapped the hood of the car the way one might pet a friendly horse. "He means what can he do for us!" he exclaimed.

"We don't need to jump over any more stuff like we did last night," said Rev, making his bottle last. "I almost tossed my cookies."

"I retain much data on needs and desires of human beings," said KARR.

"Whatcha mean?" said Rev.

"You wish, for example, to consume fuel."

"To eat, yeah."

"Along with fuel intake, you require fluids."

"Yeah! I'd like a half-gallon of good—"

"You wish to reproduce."

Befuddled, Tony and Rev looked at each other. When realization crossed their dim intellects they said, almost in chorus, *"Yeah! Reproduce, right!"*

A limitless vista of opportunity opened up inside of Tony's head. It was composed mostly of visions of solid food, potent booze, and—as he had said—wild, wild women. It seemed terrific. "So how come you were turned off in the first place?" he said.

"I was deactivated by my creator, Wilton Knight."

"The guy in the newspaper article!" said Rev. "He built you?"

"He brought me into the world and then turned me on."

"Hey, Rev," said Tony. "That Knight guy treated this car the way my old man used to treat me. You got my sympathy, KARR. We'll take care of you . . . if you take care of us, like you just said."

I am attempting to perform that function exactly. What do you require first?"

"Oh, wow," mused Tony. "A couple of eggs, sunnyside up, and some hash browns, and a mess of sausages, and—"

"I possess no eggs, or cooking facilities," interposed KARR. *"Perhaps you could direct me to the nearest chicken."*

"Oh, great," said Tony. "A comedian."

"I am not a comedian. I am KARR—the Knight Automated Roving Robot. I am the prototype of the automobile of the future."

"This guy repeats himself just like a ride in Disneyland," said Rev, who had given up trying to escape from the backseat and had settled down with the remains of his latest bottle.

"Wait a minute," said Tony. "Last night, when we busted out of the garage, there was another car outside that looked just like you. There's more than one of you—maybe a whole production line, right?"

"You are in error. I am one of a kind."

Rev stopped drinking long enough to agree

with Tony: "But KARR—I saw it too. Tony's right."

KARR's powerhouse revved with an alarming roar, causing Tony to stumble backward and sprawl in a heap before the foot bumper. Rev suddenly found that he was not so comfortable in the backseat.

"I am the prototype of the automobile of the future. I am unique."

Tony steadied himself. "Yeah, sure—whatever you say. You must be right."

"What you believe you saw could have been no more than an inferior, production-line imitation of me. A pale copy of my original and revolutionary new design."

"Touchy," said Tony. "Don't get your gaskets all steamed up."

"That reference has no meaning," KARR said stonily.

"Look, let's go back and just get us some food, huh? Forget I even mentioned that other stuff."

"As you wish."

"Tony?" said Rev. "I'm not trying to be stupid or anything, but do you know where we are?"

"Not far from the city."

"I have approximated our location on the number-two screen," said KARR, displaying a map of the northern Los Angeles area. Their location was pinpointed by a blinking dot on the map.

"I never could read maps very well," said

Rev, his bottle now dry. He chucked it out of the cabin.

"There is a good possibility that numerous purveyors of food exist within the metroplex. We shall investigate," KARR's motor engaged.

"Wait a minute, KARR," said Tony, rushing around to the driver's side. "We can't go nowhere until we find you some license plates. Without plates, they'll pick us up quick."

"You are safe inside me."

Tony was waving his hands ineffectually. "Yeah, I know, but we gotta be inconspicuous. Like, incognito. You know?"

"Why?"

"So we don't attract no attention."

"From whom?" Obviously KARR was unconcerned with the law.

Tony thought fast. "From the guys who want to take you back to that garage and turn you off again. For good."

Rev colored. "Don't get him angry again!"

"I understand your strategy," said KARR. *"We will first locate 'plates,' as you call them. Where shall we look?"*

"Just leave everything to me," said Tony.

An hour and a half later, Tony tapped on KARR's closed window and woke Rev up.

"How'd it go?" said Rev.

Tony grinned a serpent's grin and withdrew a pair of California plates with current stickers on them from the depths of his jacket.

"I hiked up the road till I got to some houses," he explained. "I found this old junker in a garage. I slipped in like a ghost and liberated them. Still too early; all the rich folks hadn't got up to get their papers yet."

"Thou shalt not steal," warned Rev.

"Don't be such a wet blanket. KARR doesn't care, right, KARR?"

"It sounds as though you proceeded in the fashion best dictated by logic," responded the car.

"Yeah, right. So anyway, I found another car in another driveway, and I pulled the old switcheroo. We got valid plates, and nobody'll notice them missing from the junker, and the car that belongs to *these* will be okay for a while, too. Nobody ever reads their plates. As long as they notice plates are still on the car, they'll never check. And by the time they do, we're all gonna be somewhere else. Got the program?"

"An efficient job," said KARR. *"And now we shall locate food for you and Mr. Rev?"*

"Right." It took Tony a few moments to screw on the stolen license plates, front and back.

He seated himself in the driver's bucket and the car said, *"Do you wish to drive, or shall I?"*

Skeptically, he eyed the wheel and the incomprehensible assortment of controls. "Why don't you go ahead . . ." he said, antsy.

Rev managed at last to squeeze his squat

bulk past the buckets and into the passenger seat. Tony watched KARR's wheel turn itself as the car backed out of the overlook's parking lot. He laughed, a little nervously.

Neither he nor Rev were fully aware they had just embarked on what the newspapers would soon be calling "a spree of crime, mayhem, and destruction."

6

Among the fashionable groupings of expensive office buildings that made up Los Angeles' west side, the FLAG building was typically modern—mostly glass and steel and hard linear planes whose mirror surfaces threw back the light of the setting sun.

Michael lounged in Devon's office, holding a copy of the police statement taken from the guard attacked at the Knight Laboratories complex the night before.

"White male adult," he read aloud. "Middle-aged, possibly as old as late fifties. Short. Stocky. White hair and brows, approximate weight one-fifty. Eyes—blue. Wearing tattered overcoat." His eyebrows went up as he read: "Unshaven, unbathed. Unbathed? I guess he smelled pretty rank." His eyes scanned the rest of the too-brief page. "Sounds like a wino, not a thief of industrial secrets." He turned to Devon, seated behind his desk making a phone call. Waving the page, he said, "Plus which the guard swears that this wasn't the guy who zapped him . . . which means the guy we want we have no description on . . . which means your prototype for KITT is in the hands of two guys—maybe more—and we don't have the foggiest idea of where to start looking for them. Great." He pitched the page at Devon's desk and missed. "I wish to hell I hadn't read that."

Devon raised his hand for silence. Michael slouched in his chair.

"Devon, will you get off the bloody phone!"

Devon murmured some excuse to the party on the other end and hung up, fixing Michael with steely eyes. "There's no need to shout."

Michael kicked out of his seat and started packing, like a caged tiger. "I want you to stop being so coy about the prototype. What is it you haven't told me about it?" He swept the air into his arms in exasperation. "Hell, even KITT smells something fishy!"

Devon removed his glasses and massaged the bridge of his nose. "The KARR program is something that I'd enjoy forgetting about, totally."

"Why don't you start at the beginning?" said Michael. "You know, with *once upon a time. . . ?*"

"When we initiated the program that ultimately resulted in what KITT is today, our first objective was to make the proposed FLAG vehicle—the technicians dubbed it the 'FLAG-ship'—as accident-proof as possible. We synthesized the alloys in conjunction with NASA to make the car's dent-proof skin. We formulated high-impact compounds the general public doesn't even know about. We were so busy making the damned thing indestructible that we barely thought about programming until we had a completed prototype."

"I don't follow you," said Michael.

"KARR's basic programming directives are quite different from KITT's," Devon said. "We derived KARR's original programming from the idea of making the car demolition-proof. Essentially, KARR is programmed to protect itself from harm at *all* costs . . . and I emphasize *all*."

"Whereas KITT. . . ?"

KITT's basic directive, as we both know, is to protect human life first and foremost. KARR has no such filter for determining its actions."

"You mean, it would mow down a crowd of people just to get out of a scrape? Something like that?"

"It's only governor is logic, and it applies logic ruthlessly. Human life doesn't matter to KARR. The only thing that *does* matter is self-preservation." Devon toyed with a pencil on the desktop.

"I'll bet this is where the Defense Department comes in," said Michael.

"Yes. Wilton Knight exhibited the prototype to the government when the time came
to secure patents. Many military officials pre-
sided at the demonstration, and they became
quite excited over the possibility that KARR's
technology could be applied to offensive land
weaponry."

"Just like that riot-control helicopter they
came up with last year?" said Michael. "That
was tested in L.A., too. No wonder they got
all hot and bothered about KARR—if you installed machine guns, you'd have quite a
snappy little urban tank."

"Wilton Knight said no. He refused the
government."

"He seemed to be a salty old dog," Michael
said, conjuring up a remembrance from the
short time he had known the billionaire. "If
anybody could tell Uncle Sam no and get
away with it, it was Wilton Knight."

"The military was developing its own equiva-
lent of KARR, anyway," said Devon. "It was
just a matter of timing—and advances that
Knight Industries had that the Army didn't."

"There were also a number of bogies in the
prototype that could only be resolved by starting all over again. Rather than pursue the
KARR affair to its acrimonious conclusion,
we began work on KITT—from the ground
up, determined that this time there would be
no mistakes or shortsightedness."

"Is that the reason why Wilton Knight didn't

just stick me into KARR and send me on my way for the Millston assignment?"

"Precisely. You would not have survived, had you been driving KARR instead of KITT."

"Seems wasteful, though," said Michael. "To just abandon one and start another one from scratch."

"That's not exactly what happened," said Devon. "First of all, certain of the components were enormously costly to fabricate. In some cases—as with many of the visual-display system, we simply removed them from one and reinstalled them in the improved model. KARR does not, therefore, have as fundamental a link with its driver as does KITT. To KARR, passengers are incidental. If everything had gone according to plan, KARR would be totally dismantled by now. Unfortunately—"

"What happened?"

"Wilton Knight came across *you*, bleeding to death in the desert with your face shot off."

It began to dawn on Michael why Devon had been so pressed for time such a short while back. Wilton Knight was dying . . . the nonlethal version of the car had to be completed . . . and his own life had to be saved. No wonder Devon had looked so harried when they had first been introduced.

"It was simpler, in all that turmoil, to just deactivate KARR and throw a tarp over it until such time as we *could* proceed according to plan. But now—" Devon held up his hands in a helpless shrug.

"We don't even have a motive," said Michael. "Could that old wino have been some kind of industrial snoop?"

"Seems too late," said Devon. "After the KARR test run, spies were crawling all over the place. Wilton Knight could only trust people he knew by sight. We finally relocated to the estate, as I've described. As far as the agencies interested in KARR knew, we took the prototype with us. No, I don't think this theft is connected to industrial espionage. As we know, no one can guarantee that there was even anybody inside the vehicle when it broke out. For all we know, the men who broke in engaged the power by accident, left the premises, and KARR warmed up on his own."

"That means we sit here and wait."

"Exactly. We wait for its hydrogen fuel stock to run out, or its power cells to deplete, and then we go pick it up."

"*If* there's no one with it."

"Yes. Putting out a blanket APB for every car of that standard make and color would be foolish. I don't think we'll be forced to that."

"Unless KARR commits some crime," Michael said.

"Yes. Heaven help us if that's the case."

"Why didn't you just blank the programming before you put the thing in storage?"

Devon sighed. "Recall events. See if you can guess."

Michael did some mental addition. "Okay," he said, enumerating items on his fingers. "The rush to get KITT finished in Reno. Industrial spies everywhere. Nobody trusts anybody. Me to deal with." He snapped his fingers. "You had to deprogram KARR personally. Wilton Knight would not have trusted anyone else, not during all the chaos the move to the estate and my own arrival was causing."

Devon dipped his head. "Very good. You win the Holmes Award for deductive logic."

"KITT said that car was—" Michael tried to recall the words. "Like a Neanderthal version of a person—animalistic, basic."

"KITT's programming is altruistic, for want of a better word," said Devon. "KARR is self-serving, devoid of conscience, and therefore, potentially very dangerous. It *learns* in the same way KITT does ... but if the people who have it—if any—or the people into whose hands KARR may fall, program it with information it deems a threat to its own existence, then they could create a menace that would very quickly exceed anyone's control."

"Devon, KITT picked up what he called sensor echoes from KARR once. I'm sure we could use that capacity to search for KARR. It's better than sitting around here waiting for a police report or a disaster to happen." Michael was on his feet again.

"I agree. Bonnie has been giving KITT a full

fueling and battery charge while we've been waiting."

Michael smacked a gloved fist into his palm. "And I agree that the sooner we get that car back, the sooner we'll all be able to sleep."

Michael found Bonnie and KITT inside the Knight Industries service truck, which was parked in a garage bay beneath the foundation building.

He entered the truck from the rear. KITT was parked in the back half of the trailer box. Past that was a computerized diagnostic center whose equipment lined the right-hand wall. Custom work surfaces projected outward for economy of space and convenient access; below the counters were sectioned drawers stocked with tools. Several TV monitors displayed KITT's various electronic idiosyncrasies in fluctuating waveforms. Machines hummed importantly. Michael also heard a beeping, heartbeatlike tone. To the left of the work area was a compact office, a duplicate of that aboard the Knight 2000 jet, with three of the usual thronelike leather chairs, carpeting, phones, more TV screens, and food facilities.

KITT's hood was up and several thick black cables snaked out of the engine bay. Bonnie was bent over, tinkering inside, one leg extended backward for balance.

"Quite a fancy spread," Michael observed. "All the comforts of home. But where do you sleep?"

Bonnie's body stiffened slightly as Michael's voice startled her. Then she withdrew from the engine bay, clearing her hair out of her eyes with her wrench hand. Her coverall was smudged with grease from her efforts to tune KITT up.

"There's a sleeper tacked onto the tractor, like with most trucks," she said, her tone icy and businesslike.

Michael peeked inside the cockpit. "How goes it, old buddy?"

"*I feel much better, thank you,*" said KITT. "*Bonnie's given me nearly a full charge.*"

"I wouldn't touch that line with a pitchfork." Michael smiled.

Bonnie stood her ground. As far as she was concerned, the mobile lab was her domain, and where KITT was concerned, Michael was still an irresponsible interloper. "What do you want?"

"Well, to chat, for one thing." Michael tried to be amiable. "For another, to pick up KITT so we can hit the beat and search for our renegade prototype."

"You've heard from the police?"

"No. We're going to try not to let it go that far. KITT can detect the presence of the other car, so we're going to cruise—"

"And hope you get lucky?" she said, hands perched on her hips.

"Well—yes."

"Nice of you to admit it."

"What?" Now he was lost.

"That you're not a hundred percent in control of the situation," she said.

"I find myself in agreement with Michael," KITT said. *"To patrol is better than sitting and waiting for a potential disaster to occur."*

"Hold still," Michael said, moving closer.

"What?" Now it was Bonnie who was taken aback. Michael enjoyed the few seconds the shoe stayed on the other foot.

He rubbed just above Bonnie's eye with his thumb. "Grease on your forehead," he said with a smile, wiping his hand clean on a bandanna.

She blushed with a surge of anger and embarrassment, retreating to the office area.

Michael felt the anger he'd experienced in Devon's office return. "What is it with you, Bonnie?" he said in a stern, loud voice. "I mean, what's your *problem?*"

"Look," she said, turning to confront him. "Let's not play games. I know your dossier by heart. You think you're quite the lady killer. Well, that brand of baloney doesn't function with this girl, so why don't you stop slicing it so thick?" Her eyes flared at him, like hot coals.

Michael turned on KITT. "This is all your fault, isn't it, KITT?" he said with irritation.

"Don't look at me, Michael," returned the car. *"I simply provide the information that is asked of me. Bonnie punched up your dossier, not me. She remarked that you would be quite*

attractive if you weren't such 'an arrogant, self-centered, egomaniacal—'"

"KITT, be quiet!" Bonnie shouted.

Michael was nodding to himself and smiling. She came abreast of KITT's hood. "All I want," she said in a smaller, more controlled voice, "is to be considered another member of the team, and not another potential victim for your long list of . . . conquests, okay? Is that so much?"

"It is if you're asking me to pretend you're not a desirable-looking woman," Michael said. "But even that doesn't mean I'm blind to your accomplishments and qualifications, you know."

"I designed this mobile lab!" she claimed, a bit desperately. "I'm responsible for helping get KITT out of the lab in time for you to rush off and dent him up in Millston! I've engineered—"

"I know," interrupted Michael. "I read your dossier too, Dr. Barstow."

The way she stopped in midsentence was a little comical.

"You're even the one who came up with the chess notation for radio calls," he continued. "You know—'Rock to Knight,' and so on? That's something Devon never would have concocted."

"Er, yes, that's . . . of course that's mine," she said, confused.

"What do you suggest we call KARR, in that event?"

"Who knows?" She moved to the equipment side of the trailer to adjust one of KITT's outputs so the wave became uniform on the screen once more. She snapped off a row of toggles that Michael recognized as power-feed controls. "*Knight Errant,* perhaps?"

"*Excuse me, Bonnie,*" said KITT. "*Unless I'm mistaken, you seem to have repositioned my main power booster.*"

They both looked at the car in surprise, and Bonnie said without hesitation, "That's right. Just carving out some elbow room for a new component."

"What kind of component?" said Michael.

Her eyes went from KITT to Michael and back again. "Just planning for the future," she said, an enigmatic gleam in her eye. "I'm not certain it's necessary, yet." She pushed the hood down and locked it into place.

"Tell me, Bonnie," said Michael. "Does KITT have any vulnerable spots? Any way to get past his defenses?"

"Absolutely not," she said—but the way her eyes went wide and her head shook told Michael that it was something she had no desire to discuss in front of KITT.

Michael nodded, silently, to show he understood. To cover, he said, "How about chinks in the armor of the cold lady scientist?"

"That's an obnoxious cliché," she said, relieved that KITT did not chase the matter of Michael's question. She was obviously working on some mechanism by which KARR might be outfoxed and deactivated—or destroyed.

"Well? Is it true?"

She pointed a thumb at herself. "*This* armor is impregnable, mister." But she was smiling at last. She flipped off some more switches with the heel of her hand. "KITT is ready to roll."

"Truce?" said Michael, still watching her.

She folded her arms. "We'll see. Meanwhile, you have a jousting opponent to locate, Mr. Knight."

"Right." He climbed into the cockpit and shut the door. He did not wait around for Bonnie to give him a favor to carry into battle.

7

The garish sign blinked furiously on and off to distract traffic, and Tony saw it.

CLOWNBURGER'S THREE-RING CIRCUS OF FOOD FUN!

"*I detect numerous purveyors of food,*" said KARR. "*Please tell me which you prefer.*"

"Let's grab the Clownburger," said Tony.

"I thought you wanted breakfast stuff," Rev grumbled.

"Haven't you heard? They do everything at one of these joints," said Tony. "Three squares a day. You never have to go anywhere else."

"Big deal. You haven't told me where we're gonna get the scratch to pay for the food." It was obvious that Rev was getting disagreeable because, like a small child, he wanted his bottle.

"Hey, with these wheels, we just light out with the grub. Convenient, huh? Go on, KARR, hit the Clownburger. I mean, drive through it."

"He means the driveway, not the building," Rev said.

"As you wish."

Both men had sat gawking at KARR's wheel turning itself throughout the entire drive. Now they hung on as the vehicle cut a wide U-turn out of the middle of the broad urban street, slicing across four lanes of traffic, heedless of the oncoming cars. Tires squealed and horns bleated angrily.

"Far out!" exclaimed Tony.

Rev held on to his seat, the blood draining from his face. "I never did like driving in L.A.," he croaked.

KARR locked brakes and skidded next to an enormous plastic head with a bulb nose and a huge top hat. It blinked on and off. In the center of its mouth was a grille for the PA speaker through which the high school kids working inside the restaurant took drive-in orders.

"No sweat," Tony reassured Rev. "When this guy wants to go somewhere, he *goes*!"

Inside the Clownburger, the kid on duty at the drive-in window heard the *ding* from the pneumatic hose that signaled a customer. He stopped studiously picking his nose and checked the mirror. A black sports car covered with road dust sat waiting.

He reached up for the microphone on the extension arm, glancing at the clock on the wall above the indoor dining area. It was a loud, round clown face. Jerry, the kid, hated that damned, grinning face—it reminded him of Alonzo, the manager, who had just left for the evening. In two more hours, Jerry could leave himself. When Alonzo wasn't watchdogging, everybody goofed off anyway—dropping the burger patties on the floor and general hijinks like that. The only reason Jerry had taken a job in a dump like Clownburger in the first place (he and his high school cohorts preferred the Burger Meister, closer to the school; it had better fries and less kid-oriented promotional hoohah) was so that he could eventually afford to buy a rig just like the one sitting in the drive now. Only he'd take better care of it—polish it and drive it around the city on Friday nights, playing Sammy Hagar tapes full blast.

Jerry hit the button and the five seconds of canned callipe music spun off. Then he went into his act: "Ladies and gentlemen! And children of all ages! Welcome to Clownburger's Center Ring! The ringmaster is ready for your order!"

The spiel was Alonzo's fault, too.

Rev was staring unbelievingly at the ringmaster head when KARR spoke: *"What is that voice?"*

Tony grinned. "That's just the ringmaster—see, Rev, ain't this place great?"

"I scan no such person as Ringmaster," said KARR in his deadly, flat tone. *"The device outside is only a primitive remote, devoid of location."*

Dummies, thought Jerry. They always pulled in and then never knew what they wanted. "I said the ringmaster is ready for your order," he said, testily.

"I'll have that breakfast thing, whatever they call it," said Rev. "But we gotta hit a liquor store after this, Tony. I'm getting a bad thirst, you know?"

"I think I want a Double Clownburger with Circus Sauce and some Sideshow Fries and maybe a Bozo-Cola. . . ."

Rev grimaced. "Ugh. You actually *drink* that stuff?"

"Hey, can I have your order or not?" came Jerry's voice from the speaker.

"Mr. Tony! Mr. Rev! This device obviously has a concealed operator, perhaps hiding nearby!" said KARR.

"We know that, KARR," said Tony.

"If he does not openly show himself, he is a potential threat," the machine announced.

"What's he talking about?" said Rev.

"You guys wanna snap it up?" Jerry said, clearing ticked off now. "We ain't got all day, and there's people lining up behind you!"

KARR said, *"There, you see? The concealed operator is becoming abusive. Blockage to the* rear indicates some kind of ambush attempt!" The engine revved noisily.

"Knock it off, KARR, please," said Tony.

"All right, wise guy, just get the hell out of the drive and let the other customers come through!"

"You will retaliate if we do not move?" said KARR to the ringmaster speaker.

Jerry was yelling now. He didn't care if he lost his job—jobs as demeaning as this were expendable. "I'll throw you out of here personally and then sic the cops on you, jerko!" Everyone else in the restaurant stopped to look at him. "Get out of here before I demolish you!" He was red-faced and sputtering.

"I record a threat and an ultimatum, my friends," said KARR.

Tony gestured helplessly to Rev. They were both in over their heads.

"Fear not," said KARR. "I will protect you."

"Hey!" Jerry yelled through a feedback whine from the speaker. "You hear me, or—"

"Brace for collision!" said KARR.

Rev wrapped his arms around his head. "Oh, Mother of Mercy, I can't bear this anymore. . . ."

KARR's rear wheels spun madly, driving the alloy bumper into the front end of the next car back, a compact Japanese import whose hood buckled on impact. Its front grille shattered, perforating the radiator, and a geyster of stem blew upward from the wreck.

Reversing gears, KARR then swerved sideways and center-punched the ringmaster mock-up. The fluorescent tubing inside the giant plastic head exploded, spraying glass and chunks of the ringermaster's face all over KARR's hood. Steam and blue electrical smoke curled up from the support post as the wiring shredded apart.

At the first sign of trouble, Jerry stomped on the burglar-alarm tripswitch. Already he was thinking that if he got his picture in the papers for blowing the whistle on some law-breakers, Alonzo wouldn't dare fire him. He'd get a raise . . . and be that much closer to his dream car. He watched KARR wipe out the ringmaster head in the driveway mirror . . . and secretly enjoyed it.

KARR backed off the wreckage. *"As I suspected, the interior of the device was unoccupied. A clever ruse."*

Tony saw the owner of the car they had just crushed heading for them, fists balled.

Rev saw him, too. "Tony, let's get out of here!"

His mission accomplished, KARR said, *"But you have not yet obtained food. . . ."*

"Never mind that!" Tony shouted. "You hear that alarm?"

"Does the harmonic disturbance have some meaning?"

Now the owner of the car behind them was pounding on KARR's shatterproof windows, yelling bloody murder.

Tony turned from the livid face in the

window. "It means the cops'll be here any minute!"

"That is a problem?"

"Are you kidding!?" Tony nearly screamed.

"KARR," said Rev. "The cops are—well, they're like a threat. We'd all get tossed in the slammer."

"Is 'the slammer' a threat to us?"

"You bet your life. Remember that dungeon you got deactivated in?"

"I will never forget it, Mr. Rev."

"Well, the slam's just like that, only worse!"

"How may we avoid the slammer?"

Tony was still shouting. "You drive like hell out of here as fast as you can go, you stupid hunk of Detroit tin!"

"As you wish."

Again the wheels spun, and this time KARR dug out at high speed. It fishtailed wildly out of the driveway and blew up the exit lane, its left side scraping a trail of sparks against the building wall all the way.

It flashed past Jerry, who jerked his head inside the delivery window just in time to avoid being decapitated. He could not read the filthy license plates on the car, but would have no trouble identifying it. It was his coveted dream machine.

KARR was doing a healthy sixty by the time it cleared the lot and jumped the curb, landing sideways in the street and peeling away in a cloud of tire smoke. Someone in a delivery truck swerved to miss the oncoming car, and broadsided a station wagon full of Boy Scouts. Within seconds there was a full-scale traffic jam snarling all four lanes. The scouts jumped out and vainly tried to direct traffic, while Jerry watched the whole spectacle from inside the Clownburger. People had left their cars and were queuing up for food. Jerry just watched, smugly, waiting for the cops and reporters to show up. Let somebody else take the orders, he thought.

The black car had vanished into the traffic like a ghost.

"Tony! Tell it to slow down! That damned restaurant must be a hundred miles back by now!"

"Only three-point-oh-two miles, Mr. Rev," corrected KARR. *"I detect no signs of pursuit or hostile action. I shall reduce speed."*

The car decelerated and blended into the traffic flow. Rev sighed. He was shaken up and as sober as Tony had ever seen him.

They rode in silence for a while, stunned, before Tony piped up, saying, "Is this a machine or is this a machine, huh, Rev? Did you see it in action back there?"

"It was rather difficult for me to ignore it."

"Bash! Wham! Like nothing was there! Like this was some kinda bulldozer! And look at the hood!"

"What are you talking about?"

"The hood, the hood!" Excited now, Tony

said, "Pull over and stop for a second, KARR. I gotta show the Rev something important."

"As you wish."

Tony jumped out and motioned for Rev to follow.

"Now—look!" he said triumphantly.

"At what?" Rev still did not understand.

"There's not a scratch on this thing!" pointed out Tony. "Look—here's where he rammed the speaker thing. This whole side should be all scraped to hell from the sideswiping he gave the concrete wall . . . the rear end should be all kicked in—you saw what it did to that other car—and *nothing*! That guy was pounding on the window; all of a sudden I get the idea that he couldn't've gotten through that window with a shotgun!"

Back in the car, Tony got the bright idea of asking the vehicle itself about its unscathed hide.

"My prow is designed for high-impact penetration," explained KARR. *"My body and chassis are composed of a revolutionary alloy that resists fatigue and breakage. The finish is molecularly bonded to the body, and is virtually indestructible. In addition, my turbo-boost function provides additional motive power that could conceivably be used for penetration purposes."*

"Yeah," said Rev. "He plowed through a steel door last night and jumped over another car by a least ten feet. I'll never forget that."

"You mean you could, like, drive right through walls and stuff on a regular basis

and you wouldn't get all ... all crushed?"
said Tony. "You'd still run okay?"

*"Do you require further demonstration, Mr.
Tony?"* said the car.

"No. No, not just yet. But eventually."

Rev looked strangely at his partner again.

There was a strange, manic light in Tony's
eyes. "Let's go get us a little car wash, first,"
he said. "Clean old KARR up. Then we'll take
care of food and booze. And then we'll make
us some plans."

They pulled into a nearby Octopus Car Wash
just as a pair of police cruisers, flashbars blazing and sirens going loudly, zoomed past in
the opposite lane, headed in the direction from
which they'd come.

Soapy water cascaded down all around
them, sliding down the windshield, as the
cleaning mechanisms went to work.

Tony held up the stolen pistol he'd kept in
his coat, and pointed to the dashboard of the
car. "Rev, between this, and *this*, anything
we want in this town is ours for the taking!"

Rev looked dimly at the dash displays. Just
as he did, something seemed to pop with an
electronic crackle. The number-two video
screen fuzzed into snow, and then went black.

"KARR, what happened?"

The machine voice did not respond.

"KARR? You still there?" Anguish twisted
Tony's face. "Oh, hell—maybe we broke it!"

"I am fine," KARR said. *"All systems nominal."*

"Then what just happened to your TV screen?"

The car hesitated before answering. Finally it said, *"My number-two video monitor was an optional function that has proven to be superfluous and unnecessary. To conserve power I have shut it down permanently."*

"Oh," said Tony. "That's smart, I guess. Energy conservation, and all that, right?"

"That's good," said Rev. "But it won't pay for the car wash. Neither one of us has any money."

"Stupid! We get outta here the same way we got outta Clownburger. And then we go cruising for bigger fish, you catch my drift. Now, here's the way I see it. . . ."

As Tony began outlining his criminal plan to Rev his eyes shone with barely suppressed greed.

Neither of them had any way of knowing that KARR had just lied to them about the blown TV screen.

8

"You're being awfully quiet, Michael," said KITT. *"Is something bothering you?"*

They were sticking with the traffic flow and obeying the laws. Michael had not engaged in his usual buddy-to-buddy banter. Part of him was still wondering why Bonnie Barstow had experienced such an overpowering negative reaction to him, but a much bigger part was worrying the KARR affair according to his policeman's instincts. This seemed to be a crime without motive, and with only a mystery wino as a suspect. The prototype had escaped with violence and then had not been heard from in nearly twenty-four hours. No incidents. No blackmail notes to Knight Industries. Nothing. It fit none of the criteria for an ordinary crime.

"Nothing beyond what you already know," he answered. "This whole sequence of events has been pretty startling. First we find out there's another car, and now we're hunting it down. I feel like I'm gunning for your—I don't know. Your dad, or something."

"Really, Michael," the car chided. *"By now you should know better than that. I admit that even I was somewhat surprised to discover that I was not the sole prototype, and that I was in fact preceded by another model. I thought I was the test vehicle, just as you are the test pilot."*

Michael tooled the car into a turn lane and hung a left at an intersection. He was vaguely thinking of heading toward Hollywood. "See? You *are* upset! Knowing about that other car is a blow to your ego."

"Not at all. Quite the opposite—it's a compliment. Instead of being that problem-ridden prototype, I am the newer, more sophisticated version. I am the vehicle chosen by both Wilton Knight and Mr. Devon."

"Come off it, KITT. You can level with me, remember? Weren't you just a tiny bit annoyed when you found out there was another car . . . and nobody told you?"

"That is not upsetting in any way," said KITT. *"There is a perfectly rational explanation as to why I was never informed."*

"Oh?" Michael scanned the traffic around him. More nothing.

"Yes. Human error."

Michael stared at the vox-box light a moment, then snickered. "I'll never understand why Devon thinks you don't have a sense of humor, buddy."

"Human error is the bogey in most information-retrieval and computing systems."

"Garbage in, garbage out . . . right?"

"Precisely. There is a disconcerting note to this whole sequence of events, however."

"That being?"

"Put yourself in my place, Michael. It is as if your world were being visited by alien emissaries, all anxious to coexist and make a good impression. Suddenly we discover that one of the alien emissaries is a violently homicidal maniac. How would you feel?"

"Except that KARR hasn't yet made any provocative actions," said Michael.

"You're forgetting his escape from the lab compound. A total disregard for safety and human life."

It was hard for Michael to ignore the bandage still on his forehead. "Yeah. I guess you're right. You still monitoring the police band?"

"Affirmative."

"KITT, I'm beginning to think that—"

"Hold it, Michael! I'm getting something!"

The audio speakers in the car came alive with static, and then cleared. Michael recognized the female voice of the police dispatcher— Annie somebody—giving a description of his own car.

". . . last seen southbound on Vincente Street following assault and leaving the scene of an

accident at the Clownburger drive-in . . . 9211
Vincente . . ."

"That's it!" Michael felt relief that something had broken at last . . . and apprehension
as to how bad it might prove to be.

He wheeled the car toward the nearest freeway on-ramp and headed for Vincente Street
at top speed.

"Tony! Slow this damn thing down!" Rev was
petrified with fear at KARR's sudden jumps
into high speed.

"Slow *what* down?" Tony yelled back at his
partner. "I ain't driving this thing!" His panic
pulled him up short of punching buttons
blindly in an attempt to turn the car off.
"KARR! You gotta slow down!"

The black car, now cleaned and glimmer-
ing—still damp from the car wash, in fact—
zoomed up behind a laggardly linen-service
truck and ducked around it with harrowing
closeness, immediately accelerating again.

"*Negative, Mr. Tony,*" said KARR. "*You
requested a high-speed departure from both the
car wash and the food merchandising establishment. I shall comply until I have ascertained
there is no threat of pursuit. I do not wish to go
to the slammer.*"

"You and your big mouth!" said Rev.

Tony was beginning to hate Rev's constant
whining. "Just shut your trap and hang on.
KARR knows what he's doing. We got us some
food, didn't we?"

"Yes, and we certainly left a lot of excited people back at that car wash, too," Rev said, covering his eyes so he did not have to watch the onrushing buildings and cars in their path. "The Bible says thou shalt not—"

"Thou shalt shut up, already."

Without warning KARR slowed to normal speed and cruised. Suddenly everything was back to normal.

"No one is pursuing us. You may now assume manual control." Two indicator lights switched places on the dash, and Tony grabbed the wheel.

His hold was disrupted by Rev, who reached across and grabbed at the wheel himself, causing KARR to swerve before Tony brought it back on track.

"What do you think you're doing!"

"I say we take these nutty wheels back to where we got 'em," said Rev. "This ain't natural!"

KARR instantly switched from his MANUAL to AUTO CRUISE. *"Negative. I do not wish to return to the slammer."*

"See what you've started, you idiot!" said Tony. "He's just kidding, KARR ... don't worry about it. Go on, change back to that MANUAL thing. Rev'll be fine." Nothing happened, and Tony said, "Come on, KARR. You can trust the Rev and me to do good by you. I told you so, didn't I?"

"Yes. I have recorded that information in my

data bank. I can trust you and Mr. Rev. You may resume control." The panel switched back.

"What we need is to do something special for Rev," said Tony.

"Have you any suggestions as to what would please Mr. Rev?" said KARR.

Tony pulled over to the curb a block and a half from a large neon sign that winked on and off in the twilight.

TORCHY'S DISCOUNT LIQUORS

"Yeah, KARR, I think I do," said Tony. "Now listen to me close. I got a plan."

He checked to ensure that the revolver was still in his coat pocket, and loaded.

The six police cruisers in the parking lot of the Clownburger restaurant attracted quite a lot of pedestrian notice. The place was surrounded with people, looking for the source of all the commotion.

Michael was able to snatch a parking slot on the street right in front of the eatery. Pushing through the milling crowd was more difficult.

People parted and he caught a glimpse of the west side of the building. His eyes followed the long furrows gouged out of the wall backward to the sputtering wreckage of the ringmaster's smashed prop head. Beyond it, a municipal tow truck was backing up to make contact with the buckled front end of the inoperative import car.

Several of the Clownburger employees were waving their hands about wildly, relating exaggerated versions of what had occurred to officers who patiently wrote down every word.

Michael felt his coat sleeve grasped from behind and turned halfway back to see another kid uniformed in a Clownburger getup. "Excuse me," he said, speaking before the kid had a chance. "Can you tell me what happened here?"

The kid was gnawing on a toothpick and stared at Michael as if he had a third eye in the center of his forehead. Michael thought he must have been staring at the bandage. Finally the kid cocked his thumb over his shoulder in the direction of KITT, and said, "Uh . . . is that your car over there'

"Yes. Why, am I parked in the red zone?"

"Yaaaahh!" the kid yelled, punching Michael hard and unexpectedly in the kidneys. Michael's knees buckled but he regained his stance as the kid grabbed one of his wrists and fought to twist it backward into a hammerlock. He was less than successful. Someone whistled, ear-piercingly.

Michael sweated his wirst out of the kid's flimsy grip and planted the flat of his hands into the kid's chest, shoving him backward. The kid sat down hard, grunting, his face beet red.

"Just what the hell do you—?" Michael began, but the kid was yelling.

"That's him! That's him! He's the one! That's his car, right over there! We got 'im, we got 'im over here!" He scrambled to his feet.

Michael looked up into the bore of an unholstered police revolver.

"Nice and easy," said the cop, a burly guy at least as tall as Michael. "I want you to slowly put your hands in the air, palms open. Do anything else and you'll come apart *real* fast."

As a former cop, Michael was stunned to hear the standard I'm-not-kidding policeman's tough-speak directed at him. He tried to smile; one side of his face twisted upward and then wilted. "Uh—officer, this is all a mistake. I—" *Stupid!* his brain roared. Wasn't that just the kind of feeble excuse people had offered him, months before, when he was in the process of making an arrest? Now the cop would just tell him to shut up.

The cop's response was to quickly pull back the hammer on the pistol and place the barrel right against Michael's temple, right next to the bandage. "You speak when we tell you to, boy. I want you on your knees for a pat-down, and I do mean *right now*!"

Auxiliary guns were drawn by the cop's partners, and they were all centered on Michael.

With infinite slowness—that was important— Michael kneeled. A booted foot shoved him onto his face, directly amid the debris of the ringmaster's plastic head. He ate plaster dust, and his lower back still throbbed from the shot in the kidneys he'd received. But he knew enough to keep quiet and let justice run its course.

"Hey Townshend!" shouted another cop. "We got calls in from a car wash and a convenience market this dude just bumped! Both within the last half hour; both within a two-mile radius!"

Townshend, obviously the officer now searching Michael while he lay on his face, said, "Yeah, well this hotshot's little reign of terror is over for today." Michael's wallet and pocket possessions were thrown into the grass on one side. "He ain't armed, but you'd better check the car out." He stood up, keeping his boot on Michael's neck.

"Aren't you going to read me your Miranda card?" said Michael. He could see Townshend's gun was still pointed at his head.

As a reply, he got increased pressure from the boot and a rather rude, blue command to lock his lips.

Michael saw the kid who had fingered him talking to another officer.

"Yeah, that's him, all right. I remember his face; I saw it in the mirror! He musta washed his car—it was really dirty when he was here the first time—and come back to the scene of the crime! Hey, be sure you spell my last name right—that's Clarke, with an *e*. Jerry Clarke." He stopped talking long enough for a newspaper photographer to snap him standing next to the cops.

The clicking sound of the cuffs locking around his wrists seemed quite loud to Michael. It looked like nothing could be accomplished until Devon was contacted.

Meanwhile, KARR was still at large out there, nearby. Somewhere.

The light-sensor across the swinging doors of Torchy's Discount Liquors ding-donged as Tony walked into the store. He'd slicked back his greasy hair and tucked in his shirt, guessing he appeared about as sleazy as the average customer in such a place.

The proprietor, a fat guy wearing an apron, shambled out from stocking the cooler, rubbing his hands together. Tony nodded at him and pretended to browse for a while.

He selected the most expensive bottle of rye on the shelf, a full quart, and followed that choice up by picking out some equally costly bourbon and scotch. A jug of cherry brandy was next, and two six-packs of imported beer.

The counterman compared the prices of the items to Tony's wardrobe and shrugged. He got all types in this place—guys who looked like they couldn't scratch up busfare playing three-card monte in the backs of the RTD buses for a double sawbuck a shot. He'd seen it happen. He bagged the merchandise, totaled the sale, and stood around waiting for Tony to produce some cash.

Tony's head was tilted; he seemed to be listening for something the clerk could not hear.

Maybe the guy was another mental case, the clerk thought. Any minute now he'd come up with a whopper of an excuse as to why he couldn't pay. Happened all the time.

"You waiting for the shockwave from the nuclear blast, buddy, or what?"

Tony looked at the man and grinned. "Sorry. Just let me dig out the old wallet." He reached into his coat, purely as a diversionary move to buy an extra few seconds. His hand blundered and the revolver fell out, clattering to the tile floor.

There came a high-pitched, turbine whine from outside, but the counterman paid it no attention. His eyes went wide at the sight of Tony's pistol, and then his reflexes carried him the rest of the way. He dropped to the floor behind the counter.

Abrutply the front of the store imploded toward both men in an aerial flood of broken bricks and pulverized glass. The decorative displays and specials arranged in the front windows vaporized with a shockingly loud and sustained noise, and then the smell of mixing liquors permeated the air. Hanging advertisement displays jigged about on their strings as though perforated by machine-gun fire. Debris flew past Tony and destroyed bottles on the shelf behind the counter as he dipped down to retrieve his fallen gun. Out of the spill from the sudden demolition poked KARR's gleaming black nose. The driver's side door sprang open.

Tony swept the bags from the counter and made for the car. Just as he did, the proprietor came back up from behind the counter with a double-barreled shotgun.

"Yipes!" squealed Rev, from the passenger's seat. He automatically shielded his head and hit the floorboards.

Tony threw the bags into the backseat of the car and dived headfirst through the door as the clerk cut loose his first barrel. He landed on top of Rev.

The blast sprayed across KARR's hood, striking multi-directional sparks as the pellets bounced harmlessly away to destroy more of the store's stock with small, crashing noises.

Tony reached out and slammed the driver's side door. He looked out the front windshield and practically down the throat of the gun as the clerk pulled the trigger.

He heard the pellets spatter off the glass and could barely believe what had happened. He slapped Rev excitedly on the back. "Hey! Bulletproof glass!" And then he began laughing.

Intrepidly, the clerk did not stop to marvel that his shots had done no damage, but quickly reloaded and pumped two more shells at KARR. The results were just as frustrating. The burglar alarms were already ringing.

Still laughing, Tony made an obscene gesture at the clerk and yelled, "Okay, KARR! Let's blow this place—and I mean *fast!*"

"*As you wish, Mr. Tony.*"

KARR's TURBO-BOOST button lit up and, instead of backing out as Tony expected, the vehicle shot forward.

The proprietor's mouth dropped open when he saw the oncoming car. The empty shotgun was chucked quickly away as he leaped for cover.

KARR plowed right through the counter, the shelves laden with liquor bottles, and the cinderblock wall behind. The building unfolded outward into the night, and KARR disappeared with a shirkening of tires, leaving the clerk to stare out through the large hole torn in the side of his store.

"You can get up off the floor now, Rev," said Tony as they tore through a hard right turn and flashed down a residential street at a steady eighty miles per hour.

Rev struggled back up into his seat. "Why the hell didn't you just back out? Mother Mary and Joseph, boy, you're gonna get us all killed to death."

"*There was too much detritus from the structure blocking my path,*" said KARR. "*Logic dictates that it is prudent for the escape path to differ from the entry path, at any rate. I chose the most logical and direct means of egress. The street was right outside. The shortest distance between two points is a straight line. Have I erred?*"

Tony patted the dashboard as the car slowed down to a safer speed and began to navigate toward the freeway. "No, old pal, you pulled that one off just perfect. Just like I told you."

"We make a pretty good team, huh?"

"It would seem so, yes, but—"

"But what?" Tony looked at the dash. One of the LED gauges was fluctuating, bouncing wildly back and forth. Then it dwindled down to zero and blacked out, leaving a blank gap in the graph pattern on the screen. "What was that? What happened?"

"There is no problem. All systems are nominal."

"Oh." Tony looked from the dead graph to the blown TV monitor screen. Maybe this bloody car was wearing out, blowing tubes and stuff, and didn't want anybody to know. Maybe he'd have to implement his plan sooner than he expected to—like tonight.

He expected another protest from Rev, but Rev already had one of the bottles from the liquor-store haul plugged into his face.

Michael leaned against one of the workbench surfaces inside the "Rook" service trailer, his eyes shining with barely restrained anger.

Bonnie acted as though she was working on KITT, making some calibration the uniformed police officer would never notice or understand. She and KITT were both eavesdropping.

The officer—not Townshend, but another man named Cook that Michael had not even seen at the Clownburger—was doing his best to tender apologies for the case of mistaken identities between KITT and KARR ... and trying not to look foolish.

Devon stood eye to eye with the policeman, patiently listening.

"I'm sure you can understand the confusion, sir," said the cop. "Between the identical cars and the employee of the restaurant's corroboration of what we thought to be the hit-and-run suspect ..."

"Yes." Devon nodded. "I undoubtably would have made the same decisions under similar circumstances. That, however, does not excuse the rough treatment Mr. Knight received at the hands of one of your fellow peace officers."

"And *feet*," stressed Michael. "Just where is that guy Townshend? I used to be a street cop myself and that dude is nearly single-handedly responsible for the crappy image the whole department has!"

Officer Cook shook his head. They all realized he was not responsible for Townshend's behavior, but they were outraged anyway and had no other vent.

Bonnie stuck her head out of KITT's cabin. "So why did that boy point the finger at Michael in the restaurant parking lot."

"Publicity," said Cook. "He wanted his picture in the papers, like a lot of nobodies."

"That points up an even more fundamental

problem we have," said Devon. "Apart from the description tendered by the guard who worked at the Knight lab complex, we *still* have no description of the thief. Or thieves."

"While we were running your boy through the system," said Cook, "we got a robbery-and-assault call. Three units responded to a liquor store called Torchy's. Man, that place was totally demolished. It looked like a tank column had driven through it, and then a bunch of Green Berets used it for a target range. You never saw so much broken glass in your life. There was even a stray dog, lapping up a big pool of booze in the middle of the floor."

"KARR again?" said Devon.

"The owner/manager identified the car and gave our artist a description of the guy who jumped into it. He says there was only one."

"Short, stocky, middle-aged, white hair?" said Michael, recalling the traits they had gotten from the Knight Industries guard.

"No. This cat was six foot, black hair, slicked back the owner said. Late twenties to mid-thirties. Brown eyes. Italian-looking. And he had a gun."

"Stolen from one of our guards," said Bonnie. "That makes us responsible for whomever he decides to shoot, as well as whatever he destroys using the prototype."

"Our security was not at fault," said Devon.

"We're not strictly answerable for their actions."

"Excuse *me*, sir," Cook said to Devon, "but if your security was up to scratch, how did a young punk and an old wino manage to rip off your multi-million-dollar prototype in the first place?"

Devon stiffened and looked uncomfortable, as though a prankster had stuck a hatpin through the seat of his trousers and he wanted no one to notice.

"Well, thanks for all your help, Officer," Michael said, with more than a trace of sarcasm.

"Maybe until we nail the stolen car, you should garage this one," said Cook as Devon followed him to the trailer door. On the stoop, he added, "Or perhaps you should paint this one another color."

"We'll take it under advisement, Officer Cook," said Devon. "Good-bye."

He nearly slammed the trailer door in rage.

"*I hope you don't take that suggestion seriously,*" said KITT, who had wisely declined to speak in the presence of the police. "*I am quite happy with basic black.*"

"The absolute cheek of the man!" declared Devon. " 'Until *we* nail the stolen car,' indeed! What makes him think that they can do anything!" He decided against stalking angrily around and dropped into one of the leather chairs, fuming.

"That means finding KARR is our responsibility, too," said Bonnie.

"I'm all for that," said Michael, too loudly, still piqued. "But where do we start looking? KITT can only detect KARR's emissions within a very limited range. And they're probably out of the bloody time zone by now!"

"Maybe not," said Bonnie. "Maybe we're giving these guys too much credit for brains, overestimating them. I think they're still hanging around. Don't ask me why."

"Woman's intuition." Michael smirked.

Bonnie immediately got frosty. "Listen, don't take your anger out on me! You had a chance to stop them and you didn't even—"

"Please," Devon interrupted, still mad himself. "Let's not start sniping at each other."

Michael surrendered. "Sorry, Bonnie—really. I'm just ticked off, thanks to that Townshend. . . ." His shoulders sagged.

Bonnie nodded. A small smile traced her lips. "That amateur sadist stomped you. You've got more of a right to get angry than anybody. And you should change the dressing on your head. That one's filthy."

Michael's hand went up to the bandage, which he had almost successfully forgotten about.

"Whatever the intelligence of these men," Devon said, "KARR is akin to a hand grenade in the hands of a teething baby. Unless we stop them, it's only a matter of time before

someone loses their life during one of these
. . . incidents." He swiveled his chair to and
fro, agitated.

*"Michael, considering the confusion of the
law enforcement officials, regarding myself and
KARR, I'll more than understand if you decide
to work without me until this crisis has passed."*

"Forget it, KITT," said Michael without
hesitation. "I had a lot of partners when I
was a cop, and I *lost* a lot of them. I'm not
losing you. I don't plan on losing the best
partner I've ever had."

Bonnie smiled at them both, touched.

"Thank you, Michael," KITT returned. *"I
naturally cannot offer such a generalization concerning you. However, I project mathematical
odds in excess of a thousand to one against my
meeting a more compatible human than yourself."*

"It helps if you're customized to my specs,"
said Michael, frankly flattered. "So, KITT—
have *you* got any ideas on how we can stop
the Mr. Hyde of the automobile industry? Any
weak spots we haven't thought of?"

"Insufficient data," said KITT.

Michael was surprised—pleasantly—when
Bonnie motioned for him to sit in one of the
chairs so she could change his dressing. He
put his head back and watched her hover
over him, and the thought occurred: Why, she's
doing "maintenance" on me . . . just like she'd
do for KITT!

"However," continued KITT, *"since KARR*

is as powerful and nearly as indestructible as myself, an obvious consideration would be that of Zeno's Paradoxes."

"Zeno?" said Michael as Bonnie swabbed at the gash in his forehead.

"The Greek philosopher," said Devon. "A scientist and teacher of Citium, 335 to 263 B.C. He founded the school of Stoicism."

"Excellent, Mr. Devon. Zeno first postulated a question of which my twin would certainly be aware."

"I flunked Philosophy 12-A, KITT," said Michael. "What are you getting at? What question?"

"What would happen if an irresistible force met an immovable object?"

"Oh," said Michael, wincing as Bonnie applied a fresh gauze pad. *"That* question."

"Like being caught between a rock and a hard place," said Bonnie.

"You're right. But the paradox is irresolvable—as far as we know, it'll never happen."

"I wouldn't say that so quickly if I were you, Michael," said Bonnie, illuminating the possibility that the winner of a KARR versus KITT conflict could not be predicted.

"Well, I think it's high time we declared war on these turkeys, whoever they are, and pulled KARR's plug permanently."

"I was hoping you'd say that," said Bonnie. She moved to the work area and pressed a button, causing a recessed niche to be revealed.

Inside was a compact, tarpaulin-shrouded shape. To Devon and Michael she said, "Attend, gentlemen, while I demonstrate what may be our solution to the problem."

9

While Bonnie was unveiling the piece of new apparatus she'd conceived to help fight KARR, less than twenty miles away Tony was helping Rev to tie one on.

The traditional habitat of the seedy pair was a bombed-out-looking tenement deep in Los Angeles Towndale section. During the 1960s and '70s, the area had converted itself from a housing district for the poor to a locus of manufacturing plants, thanks to the proximity of the then-new freeway configurations offered commuting workers. The underprivileged were gradually driven south by rezoning and the demolition of former housing areas that made way for the plants and their parking lots. Here and there in the Towndale district a leftover structure could be seen: sooty

and teetering, with boarded-up holes where
window glass had long ago been smashed out,
and "condemned" notices plastered everywhere. It was inside the ground floor of one
such crumbling building that Rev and Tony
headquartered themselves.

Within what had once been the lobby of the
Kenilworth Hotel (a charred and faded sign
attached to the lobby desk still read TRANSIENTS
WELCOME), Rev and Tony had constructed a
circle of seats purloined from wrecked auto-
mobiles, orange-crate tables covered with the
melted wax of dozens of candles, and a sal-
vaged potbellied stove to provide heat in the
wintertime. One of the water mains connected
to the downstairs rest rooms was still functional. Surrounding the "furniture" in a crude
circle were the fruits of years spent scroung-
ing for a living: stacks of aluminum cans that
would bring a penny each at the recycling
stations, tons of mildewed newspapers, junk
auto parts that might one day be cleaned and
sold, chunks of broken display mirrors, discarded scarred-up furniture, old paper bags
stuffed with magazines, and clothing stolen
from Goodwill and Salvation Army drop boxes,
and, dominating one corner, an enormous tan-
gle of at least a million rusted and useless
coat hangers (also from the building's hotel
era) that looked like a huge Art Deco dustball.

In the middle of this chaos of garbage sat
the gleaming form of KARR, looking incon-
gruous. Tony had driven it into the lobby

through a gaping section of the building's rear wall that had been punched out in 1968 by a wrecking ball. The hole was normally covered with boards and tarpaulin and to the casual outside observer did not exist.

Rev was slumped in the sprung and creaking depths of his favorite car seat, blissfully working on his third bottle of hard spirits. He made no sound, nor did he move, except to lift the bottle to his lips, make a few bubbles as he guzzled the booze, and then replace it carefully on his knee. He reminded Tony of one of those dunk-bird toys he saw once in a toy-store window, continuously dipping its beak into a glass of water, seemingly for eternity.

Tony paced and swigged from his fourth can of beer. He was waiting for Rev to pass out but would not say so. It was crucial to his plan.

Rev's protests about the uses to which Tony had decided to apply KARR had evaporated with the opening of the first bottle. Fine, Tony thought; if he didn't like it, then he could just stay out of the whole program.

Tony's boots crunched on the debris littering the lobby floor and he crossed the dingy room and found a seat inside of KARR. Another of the readout screens was behaving erratically, its red indicator spiking as though there was a power leak or a short circuit somewhere.

He knew better than to ask KARR what

was wrong: if the miracle machine wanted him to know, it would speak.

"Do you have other tasks you wish to perform?" said KARR, as though it was reading Tony's mind.

"Uh—yeah, KARR, sure. Just as soon as Rev . . . uh, goes to sleep."

"Mr. Rev is not accompanying us?"

"Naw. We don't need him for this, and he's an old man. He needs his rest."

"Mr. Rev requires recharging?"

"Something like that." Tony killed the can of beer, crushed it between his palms, and tossed it across the room to land in the pile of cans that glittered in the dim light.

"Mr. Rev is emitting white noise," said KARR.

Tony got up and checked, and sure enough, Rev was snoring drunkenly away, boozed out at last. He put a knuckle under his chin and lifted it. "Rev?" When he let the knuckle go, Rev's chin plopped back against his chest. He'd be out of it for a while.

With the pistol—still unfired, to Tony's growing irritation—adding confidence to his mind and weight to his jacket, Tony reseated himself behind KARR's dashboard and closed the door.

"Let's do it," he said, and they were off.

The Kobamitsu Merchant's Bank was one of those smaller, suburban-looking branch offices, a place with maybe three teller's slots and a single drive-up window and no twenty-four hour banking machine outside. It lacked this last, Tony knew, because Kobamitsu patrons were not the type of people to make midnight deposits or withdrawals, and they never lacked for walking-around money. If you had an account at the Kobamitsu, it represented a business or a small corporation. And when you walked up to one of those teller's slots, it was to deal in amounts that would make the average working stiff suck air like a beached carp.

Most importantly, the Kobamitsu—as a courtesy to its patrons and customers—was located off the main drags. It was secluded, as far as any bank could be and still do business. It was the perfect spot for Tony to make his first try at grabbing something more than a meal or a few pilfered bottles of booze.

The night-natter of crickets was drowned gradually out by KARR's turbine whine, building in intensity as it approached the back wall of the bank via the parking lot.

Twenty feet from the wall, KARR stopped quietly and idled.

"Okay," said Tony. "Tell me about the wall."

KARR's red sensor scanned the obstruction ahead. *"My analysis reveals the exterior wall of the building to be composed of red brick, mortared with a very strong industrial concrete mix. It is threaded throughout with wire filaments, densely patterned."*

"Alarm wires," said Tony. "We trip those

and the cops will break their necks getting here."

"*The wire current can be neutralized,*" KARR said. "*My microwave jamming system is more than adequate to defeat their rather low deterrent potential.*"

"What about the back wall of the safe?"

"*I presume you refer to the area of the wall where the density readings indicate the presence of a metal box.*"

"Yeah, right. That's the vault."

"*Past the brick wall lies a six-foot thickness of concrete reinforced with a crosshatching of alloy rods, backed by two and a half more feet of various grades of industrial steel.*"

Tony whistled softly. These guys didn't fool around when it came to separating their cash from the outside world. "Well, can you punch through it?" It was time to find out just what this machine's limitations were. "If you can't, I'll try to pick out something a little easier. . . ."

"*Analysis reveals the concrete in the back wall to be an inferior grade. Too much sand is present in the mix.*"

That was the ticket! Some union construction guys must have shortchanged the bank on materials!

"But can you break through that and the steel?"

"*My microwave jammers will exploit the fault lines in the concrete. I shall require one strike from a distance of approximately thirty yards to breach the obstruction, and a second strike to penetrate."*

Tony grinned wide and slapped his knee. They were in! Anybody might hear the sound of the crash, but the cops would take at least twenty minutes to dispatch a unit to answer a residential call, since so many of them were nuisance calls, and Tony would be causing a loud noise, all right.

As the car backed up for its first charge Tony felt something in his stomach flop wetly over.

"KARR? Nothing personal, but do you mind if I get out and watch?"

"No, Mr. Tony—I'll simply have to calculate the absence of your body weight into my strike equation."

"Terrific. I—ahh, I want to watch this."

He jumped quickly from the black racer. His door closed by itself.

All around it was dark and quiet. Then KARR's engine revved and the black shape charged the bank's rear wall at top speed.

Tony's eyes were shut the first time the car hit. Conditioned reflex made him expect to see KARR mash itself into an accordion shape of twisted junk.

Instead it reminded him of the time he had been straightening out a bent nail by hitting it with a hammer against a cinderblock. *Chink!* The block had split into two neat pieces at his feet, sticking him with his bent nail.

Practically the same thing happened to the bank wall when KARR rammed it.

An enormous fissure cleaved the entire wall in two. The flat, grating crack of impact echoed in the parking lot like a gunshot in Tony's ears, and all at once fragments of red brick tumbled out of the wall in an avalanche. KARR revved like a snorting bull about to grind a matador into paste, backed out of the fallen stone, and surged forward again.

Now Tony was running across the lot, full tilt toward the car.

The second hit was louder and different in pitch as the separating steel screamed and gave up. Clouds of vaporized concrete rolled upward. KARR was sitting with its nose inside the vault, less than a foot away from a metal shelf piled high with banded stacks of fifty- and one-hundred-dollar notes.

Tony hurdled the piles of brick and steel and began tossing double armloads of currency into the open driver's side door. There were cartloads, bagfulls, *boxes* of money just sitting there! It was more money than Tony ever could have imagined, and although his imagination was one of the most retarded of his mental faculties, it was nevertheless an overwhelming overdose of green to his eyes. Like a conditioned thief, he did not pause to marvel at it—lights were coming on inside the homes in the distance, and soon the cops would roll in—but for now he applied himself to the only task in the universe that mattered:

stuffing as much of the money as he could sling in the next five minutes into the car.

He grabbed and threw, grabbed and threw, in an insane free-for-all. KARR's backseat began to fill up with floating cash, and there wasn't a bill in the bunch that was less than a twenty, with good old Stonewall Jackson staring dourly out of the oval in the middle of the bill.

The distant cry of woop-woop sirens brought Tony back to reality. Whether they were meant for him or not, it was the signal to leave.

He stopped to cast a single glance of regret at the money he was forced to leave behind. But he wouldn't miss it long. Stuffing the last two fat wads of bills into his jacket, he jumped into the car.

"Burn rubber, KARR! Before the cops get here!"

KARR obediently backed out and executed a screeching turnaround that pointed it in the opposite direction. Then its presence in the parking lot became history.

They fired down the sleepy side streets at a hundred miles an hour, Tony wearing a loony grin plastered across his mug. After a few seconds he noticed that the wind of their acceleration was sweeping loose currency out the open window, and he thumbed the switch that put the glass up.

After KARR decided that getaway speed was no longer needed, Tony resumed manual control of the car and parked at an in-and-out market.

Inside, he purchased a cold six-pack of beer with a crisp fifty-dollar bill and stopped at the pay phone on his way back to the parked car. He let his fingers do some pedestrian work inside the bulky Los Angeles Yellow Pages and then returned to KARR.

He had ripped a tissue-thin page out of the big book and brought it along with him. He cracked open a fresh beer and took a moment to scan the page minutely.

The heading under which he was looking was "Banks."

Tony had stopped counting two hours or so ago, but it was at some indeterminate time between heists, while he and KARR drove along like any other late-night cruiser (KARR's tinted glass effectively concealed, among other things, Tony's astoundingly sleazy and thuglike appearance, which alone might have been enough to warrant a pull-over order from a passing police car) that KARR spoke again.

"Mr. Tony? Can you tell me to what end we are accumulating all this currency?"

The question surprised Tony. "Well, KARR, it's . . . it's kinda like . . . well, you know—fuel.'

"But Mr. Rev consumes his fuel in liquid form."

"Yeah, but you need the money to get the fuel in the first place."

"But I observed no exchange of specie when

you first obtained the fuel for Mr. Rev," said the car with its damnably unerring logic.

Perhaps a diversion would work. "The Rev runs on pretty low-grade fuel," Tony said. "Whereas, if we're gonna keep *you* running . . . well, you're the prototype, ain't you? One of a kind. It costs lots of dough to keep you gassed up. See what I mean?"

"When we left the Rev, he was fully gassed, as you say?"

Tony smirked, spitting beer. "Yeah, you could say that Rev was pretty gassed."

"If so," continued Karr, "if he was fully fueled, why did he not accompany us?"

"Look, KARR, it's a surprise, okay?" Tony just wanted the dumb machine to stop asking stupid questions.

"It brings up a fundamental point," said KARR.

"What are you talking about?"

"I am due for hydrogen refueling, and I shall soon require a full power-cell charge if we are to continue this type of activity. Additionally, I require—"

"Hey, no problem," said Tony. "We'll just drop a few gallons in at the nearest gas station, okay? You take regular or high-test?"

"I require hydrogen fuel, not gasoline."

Suddenly, the idea that KARR's usage might have a limit thudded into Tony's dim mind. "You mean you don't run on normal gas?"

"Affirmative. Petroleum fuel is dirty and ineffecient."

"Oh, *great!*" clamored Tony, with a groan. "*That's* why they're not hot to get us! All they gotta do is wait till you run outta fuel and then tow us *both* away! I bet you can't get this hydrogen fuel except at some special place like that place where we found you, right?" He had already answered his own question, and cut KARR's response short by asking, "How low on go-juice are you?"

"The hydrogen-fuel gauge indicates that—"

"I don't know what dial that is, dammit!" Tony shouted in frustration. "Just give it to me in English."

"At the current rate of fuel consumption I shall have adequate stocks for the next thirty-six to forty-eight hours. However, there is another problem that—"

"Never mind! We'll get you all fixed up. No problem. But we gotta do another job tonight. One more for the road, then we'll zip on back to the hideout at Kenilworth and you can cool your wheels for a while."

"A period of inactivity for a cell charge would be most welcome."

"Yeah, whatever." Tony pulled into the empty and lightless parking lot of a large metropolitan shopping center and got out. When he was certain he was unobserved, he began to transfer all the loot accumulated in KARR's backseat to the truck—emptying the hopper so it could be filled again, in a sense. A few bills drifted away on the night breeze but Tony ignored them.

He got back into the car and checked his Yellow Page. He had inscribed black X marks next to the seven bank branches he'd hit since midnight. He checked on his location—Fountain at Tranverse—and for convenience sake selected a nearby outlet of the Commerce Bank and Trust as his last strike of the predawn.

During the drive to the bank, Tony decided that he needed time to think. Possibilities were piling up, fast. He had planned to impress Rev with the accumulated loot all along, but now that KARR had mentioned that it just might run dry and poop out sometime within the next two days, he began to think differently about his future. Trying to refuel the vehicle would get *everybody* hurled into the slammer, maybe for good . . . so that was out. Tonight he'd get some newspapers and decide on one last job—a really big heist, something that, in concert with the cash he'd already amassed, would put both him and Rev in the dough for life. And if the score still proved not big enough? Well, if he could ditch the car, he could shuck Rev easily enough, too. Just plug the old dude into a bottle long enough to sneak away with all the prizes.

And after he was a rich man, there wasn't much stopping him from ripping off dear dead Wilton Knight again, at some indeterminate time in the future, was there? Maybe they'd have developed a version of KARR by then that wouldn't go sour by running out of gas.

"Okay, KARR," he said as he turned into

the parking lot of the Commerce Bank and Trust Company, Ltd. "You know the program. Let's get it over with quick and get back to our cozy little garage."

Thirty seconds later, KARR leaped into the rear wall of the bank and tore it apart, laying the vault open like a bullet piercing a soda-pop can. Tony picked his way inside and began lofting bundles of cash into the cleaned-out backseat. His hands were filthy from all the money he'd handled this night, and at this final bank he lingered longer than usual, for sheer joy of taking possession of all that beautiful green cash and making it his.

Unfortunately, as he was leaving the parking lot he was spotted by an LAPD patrol cruiser that had responded to Commerce Bank's backup alarm system. It flared into an all-out Code Three and gave immediate chase.

"KARR!" hissed Tony, knowing how to provoke the machine. "It's the slammer again for all of us unless we get away from those cops, pronto!"

KARR laid on a burst of speed in response, and the chase car shrank away behind them.

"Blow the intersection!" Tony yelled as they approached a red light. "Lose 'em!"

In the mirrors, two more police cars slid in, tires throwing off smoke, behind the first one. Their combined flashbars looked like fireworks going off.

There were few other cars on the street at this early hour and that aided rather than hidered the chase. Skyscrapers flashed past as blurs. Traffic lights were totally ignored, and if anyone dawdled in KARR's path, they got out of the way in a hurry when they saw the black street·machine coming.

"I am monitoring the communications of the pursuing vehicles," noted KARR. *"They have contrived to establish what they call a 'roadblock' exactly one-point-oh-seven miles directly ahead of us."*

Tony was by now confident in the machine's abilities and reached up to punch the AUTO PURSUIT tab. "It's all yours, KARR. Show 'em what you can do."

"As you wish."

He looked up and saw the police roadblock looming ahead: barricades, angled cop cars, cops with drawn weapons, the works. "Smart," he said. "They think they've got us boxed in."

"There is, in fact, no existing exit path," KARR observed. *"However, this does not restrain me from creating a new escape route."*

"That's what I like to hear!"

When it became clear to the officers manning the roadblock that KARR did not intend to slow down, they opened fire with service pistols and riot guns. Slugs skimmed off KARR's flawless metal skin, sparking like struck matches, flattening impotently against the indestructible glass. Tony laughed aloud.

He expected the car to plow through the jerry-rigged dam, destroying cars and mashing cops like roaches, but KARR swerved, cranking into an extreme right turn at the last possible second.

They barreled right into a gas station.

There was a crunch as the tires met and leaped over the curb, and then they were on a collision course with two rows of robotlike gas pumps. KARR mowed them down like hollow foil soldiers, and plumes of sputtering orange gasoline fanned up into the air behind them.

"That's gas!" yelled one of the cops to his partners. "Cease fire or you'll blow us all to hell!" The barrage of bullets stopped.

They watched helplessly as KARR continued, on course, through the service garage, the glass-paneled roll-up doors disintegrating around the black juggernaut and caving in.

KARR dodged around the hydraulic lift with inches to spare and punched out the back wall of the garage.

The chase cars nosed down to tire-wrecking halts in order to avoid wiping out the barricade and a bunch of fellow officers. They were all out of the race.

The garage workbench flew apart, pitching tools everywhere before the cinderblock wall split apart into gravel. KARR hung a violent left and vanished up a narrow alleyway, showing no tail lights at all.

The officers could do nothing except watch all the rubble settle and dust clouds rise. A support pole to one of the canopies covering the pump area, which KARR had clipped on its way into the garage, bent double and brought the entire canopy down with a reverberating crash of aluminum. Fresh gasoline was flooding the pavement and running off the curbing by now.

And KARR was gone.

Moments later, after backup units and the fire department were summoned, the phone began to ring in Devon's office at the foundation.

KARR found its way back to the Golden State Freeway on its own, while Tony swilled the last of his brew and fingered the cash distributed all over the backseat.

"Ya did real good, KARR. Excellent." Might as well start the whitewash now, Tony thought. "And we'll be taking care of all that stuff you need as soon as we pull one more job, but don't fret that, because that's tomorrow. You know how to get back to the Kenilworth from here?"

"*Affirmative.*"

At that moment, breezing southward with thousands of dollars all around him, Tony felt truly unstoppable.

10

"We all know just how indestructible the alloy that coats KARR—and KITT, of course—is," said Bonnie, pulling the tarp free from the shape on the workbench. "There's virtually nothing that could damage or stop either car. Hardly anything, that is, except this."

The device certainly looked complicated, incorporating a lot of baffles and glass—or plastic—along with coils and tubes. There were no perceivable control mechanisms, at least on the outside.

Michael moved up for a closer peek. "Looks like a neon barber pole," he said.

"It's a resonating laser, Michael," said Devon, rising from his chair. "I'll leave it to Bonnie to explain to you exactly the purpose we intend to put it to. I don't wish to go through it all a second time. I'll be in my office if you need me."

After Devon left the trailer KITT said, "*I believe Mr. Devon finds the idea of destroying or incapacitating something he labored years to create ... distasteful.*" After a beat KITT added, "*And I must confess I feel much the same way, having my weak spots exposed. I'm not supposed to have any weak spots. . . .*"

"Of course, we have KARR's deteriorating component integrity," said Bonnie. "But it's foolish to depend on that because it's unpredictable. The resonating laser represents the only form of direct, practical action we can take."

"That is, without dropping a nuke on it," said Michael. "How does this thing work?"

"The front scanner is the target," she said, walking over to KITT and running her finger along the red sensor vent in the hood. "The laser is powerful enough to put a burst of energy directly into the scanner and cause it to blow. This is the only vulnerable spot, and it's protected by a grille of the same alloy that sheets the car."

"So it needs to be a dead-on shot," said Michael, mulling it over.

"Put that shot in here"—Bonnie tapped the scanner, her other hand in her coverall pocket— "and you'll render all of KARR's other systems inoperative. It will become an immobile hunk of metal."

"That's it?"

"That's it. The laser will be mounted in the bay I've provided inside of KITT, forward-aimed and coordinated with a visual targeting device on one of the monitor screens."

"You sure you'll be able to fit that thing in?" said Michael.

"The gap left by shifting my power booster seems to have left a more than adequate space," said KITT.

"What about the targeting device? Sounds a bit too much like a video game to me."

"It'll be easy," said Bonnie. "Watch."

She flipped some toggles on the console and machinery began to hum and vibrate. There was a faint, high-pitched noise. Bonnie moved to the end of the bay containing KITT and pulled down a chainfall, sweeping it to the opposite end of the trailer box. From it she hung a two-by-two plate of steel. It revolved lethargically on the end of the hanging chain.

"You need to keep the laser on target for two full seconds for maximum results," she said, and then hit a red button on the console.

The pencil-thin glass nose filled up with ruby light and the metal on the chainfall began to smolder in the center. It continued to turn on the end of the chain, and its own motion caused the laser beam to slice it neatly in two. The bottom half clattered to the floor of the trailer and Bonnie switched the machinery off.

"Two seconds? And I have to be parked in

front of KARR for that long to do it?" He
looked from the laser to the plate and back.
"I'm beginning not to like this a whole lot. . . ."

"Also, Michael, you have to fire the laser
from a distance of one hundred yards. Or less.
And your beam has to stay on target for two
full seconds to be sure you knock out the
scanner and—if the grille gets in your way—
that random drift will carry the beam into
the scanner facets for at least part of those
two seconds." She was standing now with
arms folded again, most of her humor gone.

Michael paused to calculate and then knew
why she was so grave.

"Wait a minute. KARR isn't going to sit
around, parked, waiting to get blasted, so it's
reasonable to assume that at some time I'll
be driving toward it head-on. That's when
you want me to take my shot?"

Bonnie did not nod.

"And KITT—and therefore KARR—can cover
that one hundred-yard minimum range in . . ."
His heart went *thump*. "In just about two
seconds flat."

*"One-point-nine-nine-seven seconds, provided
the road is even and flat,"* corrected KITT from
behind him, dryly.

"Thanks. I'm really relieved."

"There's something else, Michael," said
Bonnie.

"Good news or bad news?" Michael shot
back. "Ahh—forget I asked."

"The laser—this version, anyway—is only good for one shot."

"Wonderful. Michael the guinea pig strikes again. I really have to hand it to the technical resources of Knight Industries. Chalk up another point for versatility...." He shook his head wonderingly. "God."

Bonnie waited a beat for him to stop talking and then said, "Are you finished?"

"What?"

"Are you done with your tantrum?"

A tiny snort escaped him. He had to smile at that. "Yeah. I guess so. If I don't do it, nobody does it. And I hate the idea of not being indispensable."

"I figured," she said, softening.

"The idea of uniqueness appeals to Michael, Bonnie," said KITT. *"He is rather like me in this single respect. His psychological profile indicates a strong tendency toward—"*

"Let's not get into my psychological profile again, okay?" said Michael. To change the subject he asked, "What about the people inside the car when I zap it with the laser?"

"Once the scanner is burned out they'll come to a rather jolting stop, but KARR's own construction ought to keep them from getting harmed. You should be able to arrest them intact."

"I don't do arrests anymore," he said. "Let those gung-ho Los Angeles cops do the paperwork." He resumed his seat. "All right. It sounds feasible. Crazy, but feasible. And what happens if I miss?"

"Perhaps then your question concerning Zeno's Paradoxes will be answered," said KITT. *"At my risk."*

"Oh, *really?"* said Michael, snidely.

"Correction. Our risk."

There was a soft, burring ring, and Bonnie moved to pluck a phone receiver from a console. "It's Devon. He wants us to get up to the office right away. KARR has gone on the rampage."

"All over the city. I've hardly been off the phone," lamented Devon as Bonnie and Michael congregated around his desk.

Behind him was a broad pull-down street map of Los Angeles, minute in detail and covering the area from Pasadena to western Beverly Hills, from Griffith Park at the north end to Los Angeles International Airport at the south end.

"We already know about the misadventure at the Clownburger and its aftermath. KARR was seen at the Octopus Car Wash seven blocks away, the in-and-out market a mile and a half from there, and, of course, the liquor store that got demolished."

"Torchy's," said Michael.

"Yes." Devon had a palmful of little black push-pins, and began to note each location on the map by impaling it. "It did not take long for the aspirations of our unknown thieves to become more grandiose. Here." He shoved a red pin into the map. "The Kobamitsu Merchant's Bank, several hours ago. Eighty thousand dollars in cash taken, the safe and rear wall destroyed. No traces."

"While driving KITT," said Michael, "it's easy to fantasize about what kind of crimes you could commit if you had the resources he has."

"From all indications, the thief drove through the wall, loaded the car with money, and left. Not that there's a police car that could catch or hamper KARR's progress. But less than twenty minutes later ..." Another red pin dotted the map several inches from the first one. "The Central California Trust main branch. One hundred and twenty thousand dollars. Same *modus operandi*."

"I begin to feel we are in deep trouble," said Michael stiffly.

Devon inserted a third pin. "Golden State Savings and Loan, thirty-three thousand dollars." Another pin; the map was beginning to look like a World War II guide for a bombing mission. "Security Nakajima Bank of California, forty-five thousand dollars plus several giveaway gold railroad watches—part of a bank promotion. Patriot Savings, fifty-one thousand dollars. At that one KARR went in the back and out the front, totaling the building."

Devon seemed almost fatalistically overcontrolled. "This is all one night's work. KARR's microwave jammers allow it the capacity to defeat or confuse most conventional alarm configurations. It monitors the police bands, and even if the police catch up to it—"

"What can they do?" said Michael. "Nothing. I know."

Devon's desktop phone system rang again. All three looked guiltily toward it. Bonnie nervously wiped her palms on her jumper. Michael knew that all she could think about was the fact that she, like Devon, had helped create the vehicle responsible for a one-car crime wave.

Michael wandered around the office, embarrassed to listen to Devon dissembling over the phone, employing his vast reservoir of diplomacy and tact to calm the agitated caller. Michael would be cursing, threatening, and racking the receiver with anger. His built-in nonsense filter did not allow for soft-soaping people who were abusive. His characteristic method was to double the abuse and hurl it back the way it came.

Devon hung up with a pained expression.

"How bad?" Michael said.

"I hadn't yet finished with the *other* banks he hit," Devon said, staring absently at the desktop. "But he just now cleaned out the Hollywood branch of the Commerce Bank and Trust. The police responded, gave chase with three units, and set up a roadblock—they tried a cul-de-sac trap."

Michael's mouth stalled in the open mode.

The cul-de-sac was a classic mousetrap ploy, where you coordinated chase units to make your suspect run into a box from which there was no exit. He'd pulled it off numerous times both as a street cop and as an undercover detective.

"KARR slipped through with absurd ease. It totally destroyed a gas station in the process. The police firing line at the roadblock had about as much effect as an army of kindergarten kids using water balloons. KARR has vanished again."

Michael hated seeing Devon like this. To Bonnie he immediately said, "How long to mount the laser inside of KITT so it can be fired?"

"Well . . . if I don't stop for coffee . . ."

Devon looked up at her, and then at Michael, some of his characteristic deadpan calm returning. "An hour?" he said.

Bonnie made the A-OK sign with her thumb and forefinger. "Forty minutes; no sweat."

"I'll bring you the coffee personally," said Michael. "And if you need some kind of assistant grease monkey, I'm at your disposal."

"Why thank you, Mr. Knight," she said grandly.

"If you think I'm a hard taskmaster," said Devon, "you obviously haven't been around when Bonnie starts giving orders. You're about to earn your keep, believe me."

Bonnie was already on her way back to the trailer, and KITT. She paused at the door to

Devon's office and said to Michael, as she was leaving, "Two lumps, no cream. And hurry it up, mister." Then she was gone.

Devon and Michael exchanged wary glances.

Michael considered the pattern on the map. It was not consistent, and therefore it was foolish to try and triangulate KARR's hiding place from the banks that were marked as victims.

"Devon? How likely is it that KARR will just run down due to component malfunction?"

"Difficult to say. If you had asked me before, I would have told you I was certain the hydrogen fuel tanks were drained before KARR was mothballed. I was obviously mistaken. And it pulled a full-power charge before leaving the old lab facility. I'm afraid the laser may be our only option, for now."

Michael stared hard at the map. "Yeah. Now all we have to do is find them."

11

Tony woke Rev up by dumping money all over him.

By the time Tony and KARR had completed their night's "shopping," they had collected an abundance of bills of all denominations, and Rev opened his eyes to a billowing cascade of singles, Lincoln notes, sawbucks, double sawbucks, bills with faces he had never seen before, like Ulysses S. Grant and good old Ben Franklin, all fluttering down before his stunned eyes like leaves from a shaken tree.

"Surprise, surprise," Tony chanted, flipping wadded handfuls of currency into the air around his head.

"I have got to be dreaming," Rev said, slowly and thickly. 'Either that, or I've died and gone to heaven at last. Blessed are the meek, for they shall inherit the bucks." He plucked a stray fifty from his lapel and stared at it the way a small child would gape at a meteorite.

"It's real, Rev!" Tony shouted. "It's heaven, all right!" He capered around, chucking more cash and watching it float.

Rev walked over to KARR, bills spilling off him, and patted the fender. "Jalopy heaven, right, KARR? I bet you're responsible for all this ... bounty." Rev seemed to have forgotten his qualms from earlier in the evening in the face of so much cash.

"I am unfamiliar with your reference," said KARR. *"However, celebration in the face of problems seems inappropriate."*

"What problems have we got?" said Rev. Across the burned-out Kenilworth lobby, Tony's cheerful air staled a bit at KARR's words.

"I have pinpointed progressive erosion of the component integrity of my Beta and Lambda circuits. My hydrogen fuel will be depleted in—"

"Yeah, yeah," said Tony, cutting in. "We know about your hydrogen fuel." To Rev, he added, "It started squawking about needing parts and crap a couple of hours ago. And he's running out of gas."

"So?" said Rev. "You got enough dough here to buy an oil refinery."

KARR's previous explanation about the hydrogen fuel was beyond Tony's ability to encompass. "Normal gas don't work," he said.

"It needs some kinda fancy stuff, like what you'd get at that laboratory."

"*The fiber-optic elements in my scanners have suffered a twenty-four-percent reduction in opacity,*" continued KARR. "*I have also analyzed the random burnout factor that is crippling several of my functions, such as the number-two monitor screen and my vital-signs monitor. There is a seventy-two-percent probability that this trend is due to my long incarceration and the inactivity experienced during that period. There is an eighty-percent probability that more functions may short out or eliminate themselves at random if corrective measures are not immediately employed to terminate the malfunctions.*"

"You mean, like, your brakes might go out . . or something?" said Rev.

"*My power-cell storage chambers have begun to decay. They have become unstable. That is the worst of the potential malfunctions. Simple braking seems fairly secure.*"

"What happens if your power things keep leaking?" said Tony, interested now.

"*Forty-percent probability of detonation,*" said KARR.

Tony's face went cheesy white. "You're gonna blow up?"

"*Not today. But unless the defect is corrected, there is, as Mr. Rev would say, a fifty-fifty chance of explosion.*"

"I can walk," said Rev. "It's good to be a pedestrian, to stroll, and take in the sights of God's green—"

"Shut up," said Tony. "Okay, KARR, so you need a tune-up or something. We'll see what we can do for you."

"*I require the services of an experienced cybernetic technician.*"

Tony sighed. "I bet we can find one of them the same place we could find us some hydrogen fuel, right?"

"*We have seen a production-line model version of myself. Though as an imitation it is probably less durable or complex than I am, it seemed to be in peak operating condition. Therefore, someone must give it periodic maintenance. Our most logical course would be to locate the individual who cares for the other car.*"

"Right, sure," said Tony. "I was thinkin' the same thing, KARR." He hadn't been, of course, but he had no desire to look stupid in front of Rev.

"*We shall find the technician and bring him here,*" said Karr. "*After that, I will be more able to put myself at your disposal.*"

"You can't do it, Tony," said Rev, his voice dropping in pitch. Suddenly he sounded skittish.

"*There is a problem?*" said KARR.

Rev turned to the machine. "Yeah! It's called kidnapping!"

"*Your terminology is once again unfamiliar. The only relevant fact is that I require skilled service.*"

"Tony, can't you talk to this damned thing?" said Rev. "Reason with it? We can't just—"

Tony snared the arm of Rev's overcoat and dragged him over to the circle of threadbare car seats and junk. His teeth were clenched. "You're getting a conscience kinda late in the game, you know that?"

Rev slumped into a chair. A half-empty bottle of rye was tucked next to an armrest, and Rev unscrewed the cap and drew off a long, blissful slug to calm himself. "Hey—I know I ain't no saint, neither, Tony . . . but nothing we've done so far has really *hurt* nobody. . . ."

"Speak for yourself. I coshed that guard at Wilton Knight's joint, didn't I? And what about that guy we almost wiped out escaping from the garage? And what about all the freakin' property damage? No way, José; you're as guilty as I am. You're an accessory."

"Yeah, yeah, I know that, Tony boy," Rev whined. "But you just tapped that guard. I mean we ain't killed nobody yet, at least." He took another swig from the bottle and wiped his lips on his coat sleeve.

Tony thrust his hands violently into his pockets to keep from slapping Rev around. Couldn't the moron see that the things they did to live, legal or not, had to be done? That it was an us-versus-them situation? They could do what they could to keep folks from getting injured, but when it came down to it, the world hurt people anyway. Why shouldn't they benefit from it, since somebody had to? Here they'd finally gotten a break, and Rev was complaining. Maybe he'd become a derelict booze hound because he'd decided long ago that he was useless and would never get a chance to taste the good life. Tony was fond of Rev, but his convenient pocket moralizing was getting real tiresome real fast.

He was still carrying on. "Now you're talking about just *grabbing* somebody and—"

In a rare burst of lucid planning, Tony managed to put facts together in a crafty way. KARR was getting to be on its last wheels. Rev was complaining. Now if Rev thought that Tony could get KARR's technician in some aboveboard way—heavy bribery, for example—then Rev would shut up and KARR would stop beefing. And after one more score, a big one, he could cut them both loose to fend for themselves. Let them find out just how vital old Tony Cox had been.

This is what Tony thought. What came out of his mouth was, "Relax, Rev, relax. I ain't no kidnapper. I'll get KARR what he wants. Just cool down."

"No grabbin' people?" said Rev.

"Naahh," Tony said broadly. "Nothing to worry about." Drawing Rev aside, he added, *sotto voce:* "That thing talks real fancy but he's about as smart as a toaster. I'll buy him some spark plugs and stuff and he'll be happy— you'll see. After he's spiffed up, I got just one more job planned, one that won't hurt nobody. And then it's flyin' down to Rio for you-o and me-o." He slapped Rev on the shoulder. Dust rose from the overcoat. "What do you say, partner? Is that a fair shake, or what?"

Rev squeezed his eyes and was silent for a moment. It was the closest he usually came to coherent thought. "Yeah. I like that idea lots better, Tony. I just don't want to hurt people. It's ungodly, y'know? Thou shalt not—"

"Yeah. Listen, you finished off your bottle, and I'll go break the news to motor mouth."

Rev dutifully retreated, clutching his quart.

Tony smacked his hands together, rubbing them as he approached KARR. "Okay, pal, you say you need yourself a technician, then let's go get you a technician!"

By the time Tony and KARR left the building, Rev had once again slipped into a blissfully drunken stupor.

Devon had pulled down a light-board for blueprints, and somehow not seeing that Los Angeles map with all the pins stuck in it reassured both him and Michael. He was attempting to make Michael more comfortable about the use of the laser Bonnie had developed by explaining it—the elimination of nervousness through boredom principal, as Michael might have termed it.

"One advantage," Devon said, sweeping his hand across the plans clipped to the lightboard. "Once the laser is calibrated by Bonnie, it can be fired either by you or you can tie it into KITT's computers—as is the case with the joystick control for targeting."

"You mean I should just pretend I'm playing Donkey Kong instead of wiping out KARR, is that it?" Michael picked up the manual targeting apparatus and toyed with the little throttle. "So I can run KITT on automatic and fire this myself, or drive and hope my aim is better and let KITT do the shooting, right?"

"In a situation with no options, it's good to have a choice, at least," Devon said cryptically.

"Or the illusion of it, anyway."

"We must be pragmatic, Michael," said Devon. "We have to go hunting. It's too much to hope that KARR will simply drive into our arms and give up."

"The car isn't robbing the banks, Devon. It's just a tool . . . just like KITT, although I admit I have a hard time thinking of KITT as a nonsentient machine."

"So do I," admitted Devon.

"He kind of grows on you. But we're really after the guys who crowned Derek Scott, the guard, and stole the car. It's no different from a thief who rips off a pistol and uses it to commit a crime—except in this case it's one hell of a fancy pistol."

"Bonnie should be ready by now," said Devon. His hand moved for the phone console just as it rang—or more properly, twittered. Devon maintained an intense dislike for jangling phone bells, and had a substitute alert system installed.

"Speak o' the devil," said Michael as Devon answered.

He said simply, "It's ready," and hung up. "Bonnie expects you in the trailer in five minutes."

"Here I go, then," Michael said. "I don't know what bothers me more about this—the fact that it's a long shot, or the fact that I'm dumb enough to try it."

"Long shots seem to be your natural habitat," observed Devon, smiling.

"Wish me luck."

Devon nodded, like a king bestowing favor on a subject.

"Okay, me bucko," Bonnie said, pulling out from beneath KITT's hood and straightening. "You're set."

"I must confess that incorporating a weapon into my structure is a little disconcerting," said KITT.

"Don't worry about it. It comes out as soon as you and Michael put a stop to KARR."

Neither of them added the possibility that the mission might not succeed. There was nothing positive to be gained by bringing it up anymore.

Bonnie racked her tools and wiped off her forehead. It had been very close work. "You can report directly to the lot. Michael should be on his way down from the top floor by now."

"Fine. I'll see you later, Bonnie."

"Take care," she said, and watched as KITT backed smoothly down the trailer's retractable tire ramps. When he was out, and making his turn, she added, "Both of you."

Her part seemed done, but she knew she would get no sleep until the whole KARR affair was resolved. A bite of food struck her fancy, and she rummaged around in the trailer's kitchen unit. Her search was rewarded with some cheddar cheese, crackers, and a diet soda. She took her snack to one of the console chairs, and after sitting down, donned one of the mike-headphones used for phone conversations and plugged it into the stereo. She relaxed as her head filled up with Joni Mitchell.

She never heard the screech of tires outside.

Lights flashed on the ceiling of the trailer, and when her eyes opened she saw KITT's familiar red sensor bounding up the ramp.

Must've forgotten something . . . was all she had time to think.

Then she saw the stolen license plate mounted under the sleek black car's nose.

That's not KITT!

She tried to stand up quickly, but the headphone wire restricted her as the car door was kicked open.

Then Tony was on top of her.

Devon's phone began twittering again as soon as Michael was out the office door. Fearing more bad news, he hesitated to pick the thing up—but his sense of responsibility allowed him to hesitate for just one ring.

A breathless voice on the other end of the line gasped, "Mr. Miles! We tried to stop it but it ran the main gate just about thirty seconds ago!"

"What ran the main—?"

"The car, Mr. Miles, the *car!*"

Devon sucked in a panicked breath. "Why aren't the intruder alarms sounding if the checkpoint's just been breached?"

"It hit the guardpost on the way through the gate!" said the sentry. "The phone in there is under a bunch of debris!"

Suddenly, Devon realized that KARR was using its microwave jammers to kill the automatic alarms that should have sounded at the first sign of trouble.

"Where are you now?"

"Ground-floor lobby, sir."

"Where is the car?"

"I don't know, sir, but I've rung for backups. He may have gotten in but he's not going to get out!"

Devon did not bother to inquire as to just how the guard intended to stop a car with KITT's capabilities. He racked the receiver and pressed the stud on his wrist comlink.

"Michael! Michael, are you receiving me?"

Silence. Devon slapped the desktop in frustration. He'd noticed Michael was wearing the comlink; perhaps he'd forgotten how to work it.

"Michael!"

"I'm here, Devon," came Michael's voice, tinny and metallic, coming from the comlink speaker. "I pressed the wrong button on this thing."

"Where are you now?"

"In the elevator, on my way down to the garage."

"KARR has just run the checkpoint and is somewhere on the compound!" He thought he could feel Michael's immediate frustration at being stuck in the slowly descending elevator car.

"Devon, I'm putting you on hold!" Michael said.

Devon punched buttons on his console and the comlink but found himself—just as frustratingly—cut off.

Inside the elevator, Michael activated the comlink again. "KITT! Where are you?"

"I'm waiting down in your parking space, Michael," came the response from the car. "Where else would I be? We're ready to—"

It was obvious that KITT had not received Devon's transmission. "Just listen, KITT," said Michael urgently. "KARR just showed up and wiped out the guardhouse. He's somewhere on the foundation grounds. Meet me outside the ground-floor lobby!"

He glanced up to the numerals across the top of the elevator door. Four clicked over to three with agonizing slowness.

"Come on!" Michael said, smashing his hand into the door as if to spur the machine to greater speed. *"Come on!"*

"Come on, babe, you and I are taking a joyride," said Tony with a leer as he caught Bonnie's wrist in an iron grip.

She was halfway out of the chair, and when she saw him coming she grabbed the knife she had been using to slice her cheese, swinging it wide and flat to convince him that putting his hands on her was a terrible idea.

Tony saw the blade coming. He had seen enough knives bound for his body at different times in his life that this one did not scare him in the least. He pulled his stomach back, avoiding Bonnie's first tentative stab, and, maintaining his grip on her wrist, backhanded her savagely across the mouth.

Bonnie recoiled from the blow with such force that the headphone cord snapped out of the socket and the headset dropped around her neck, loosely. Sparks swam upward in her vision. All she was aware of after being slapped was the voice of the greasy goon who had done the hitting, yelling now. The words did not register in her brain, which was still reeling. She tasted blood in her mouth.

Tony twisted Bonnie's arm into a hammerlock and knocked the knife away from her other hand. It went spinning into a corner.

"Real tough little broad, huh?" he said, enjoying her struggles. "Like to play rough? Well

Tony plays rougher than anybody! You fix up KARR over there and maybe we'll find time for some fun and games!"

He shoved her forward and wrestled her into KARR's open door. "Don't let her out!" he yelled, and the door lock on the opposite side immediately clicked.

Bonnie no sooner hit the seat than she began to flail with both fists, pummeling the thug who had jumped into the car beside her.

Tony smacked her again, hard, and her head bounced off the window. When she opened her eyes, she was looking down a gun barrel.

Tony jammed the revolver into her face. "You're real cute, honey," he growled. "But do me a favor. Knock off the boxer crap or I'll spread that lovely face all over the inside of this car!"

Shaken, Bonnie desisted and shrank into the corner of the cabin next to the passenger door. There was no way she could disengage the lock and jump free, since her assailant had used a voice command to trap her.

"KARR! Let's move, now!"

"*As you wish.*" The vehicle's usual response, but now it sent a thrill through Tony. Whenever the car said that it always unpacked some fancy moves.

They backed off the trailer ramp and turned around. Seventy yards away was a chain-link hurricane fence surrounding the boundaries of the foundation property.

"The shortest distance between two points, right KARR?" Tony laughed.

KARR's wheels spun and it raced for the fence at full speed.

Michael ran out of the foundation lobby just as KITT pulled up to the glass doors.

"Michael, I'm definitely registering KARR's unstable emissions and interference output. It's exactly like an electronic fingerprint."

"Where?"

"Off the east end of the compound, and accelerating."

"That's where the trailer's parked!"

KARR never made it to the chain-link fence. Bonnie saw an opportunity and reached across, giving the wheel a spin, and the car revolved laterally with an insane shrieking of tires.

"Damn!" shouted Tony, reaching across and catching her throat in his hand. "No more!"

KARR was stopped dead in the middle of the expanse of concrete.

Inside KITT, Michael shouted, "Go!" and the distance between the two identical black cars began to decrease.

Tony yanked the wire free from the headset around Bonnie's neck and began to bind her hands to the inside door handle. The threat of the pistol was ever-present. "No more funny business, lady," he said between breaths. "Or they'll have a hard time even finding your pieces. You just simmer down. You do what I want, and you get to finish your life. Understand?"

Bonnie, having considered in a flash all the horrid implications of Tony's command, nodded, frightened.

"Vehicle approaching," announced KARR.

Tony glanced up and saw KITT headed toward them, sliding to a smoking halt less than ten yards away. A tall, rangy guy in a black leather jacket had already leaped from the car, which was identical to KARR, and was running toward them.

Michael had no idea why KARR had stopped suddenly, but his instincts propelled him from KITT and toward the enemy vehicle at a dead run. He saw Bonnie inside, struggling with a guy who matched the description given to the police after the liquor store had been torn apart.

"What're you waiting for, stupid machine!" shouted Tony. "Move it!"

The AUTO PURSUIT light winked on.

Michael was halfway between the two autos when KARR charged, like a metallic, angry bull. There was no place to run.

KARR was doing about twenty-five and gaining when Michael jumped up to sprawl across the hood, his fingers seeking the vents just below the windshield to stabilize himself.

"Faster!" said Tony, staring at Michael's grimacing face less than a foot away. "Shake off this clown!"

The red neon numbers on the speedometer

piled up to fifty, then seventy-five as they crunched across the curbing and headed in the direction of the main gate—the way they had originally come.

Michael hung on. Bonnie was shocked speechless. KITT wheeled quickly around and gave chase, but KARR had the surprise head start.

Devon burst out through the lobby doors as the two cars raced for the recently demolished gate. Several guards had their service pistols drawn.

"Don't shoot!" he ordered. Then he made out the figure of Michael clinging to the hood of the lead car, jerking crazily about as the car swerved to shake him off. The car following them was driverless.

The guards hurriedly cleared out of the path of the oncoming cars.

As the ENTRANCE drop-gate had only moments before, the EXIT gate disintegrated as KARR charged through it at a flat eighty miles per hour. The incline of the drive and the impact threw Michael up into the air. His finger muscles ached as he tried to hang on to the front of the car. Momentum flipped him over and he landed on KARR's roof with a crash that caused both passengers to flinch. Now onrushing air was blinding him. But he hung on.

KARR slid wildly into a speed turn, breaking the grip of Michael's right hand. He yawed precariously, almost falling off. He punched the comlink and screamed for KITT.

Quite clearly, he heard KITT's voice say, *"Right behind you, Michael."* KITT'S gleaming black prow was inches from KARR's rear bumper.

"That's great, buddy," gasped Michael. "Because I can't . . . hang . . . on . . . any—"

Michael's left hand slithered free and for a stomach-plunging micro-second he was in a kind of horizontal freefall, certain he would be ground to jelly on the pavement below. Instead, he thumped heavily off KARR's rear deck and smashed immediately into KITT's windshield, wrenching his back. Inertia mashed him against the glass.

KITT dropped speed at once and pulled out of traffic. His programming to protect human life offered no other option. Michael slid off the hood and placed his feet on solid ground, relieved at his miraculous rescue.

"Thanks, old buddy," he breathed.

KARR had disappeared.

12

Bonnie was overworked. Virtually the entire night had been spent installing the laser into KITT, and then had followed her abduction and the brief, mad chase . . . all as she had been sitting down to relax for the first time in over twenty-four hours. And now she was hard at work again, on KARR.

She had tried to remember the circuitous route KARR had taken back to Tony's hideout, but the twists and turns and the constant threat of Tony's pistol had blurred her senses. She had recognized none of the local landmarks and had no idea where she was being held captive. The only clear image she retained was of herself, yelling for Tony to stop the renegade Knight Industries vehicle for fear of killing Michael, who was hanging on to the roof at the time.

Tony, clearly enjoying the plight of the interloper on KARR's roof, had turned to her and with an oily, venomous voice, said, "Calm down, sweetheart, or I'll do the same for you."

She had stared dumbly at the pistol, realizing that he was threatening to kill her. The chilling simplicity of the whole situation caused some of the fight to drop out of her.

She had been given some rusting, greasy tools and commanded to work on KARR. And now she was fighting off sleep with equal parts of anger and fear.

Sunk into the workings of the dashboard, her face was inches away from a readout screen. Beneath the panel she twisted a screwdriver and watched as the numbers adjusted upward.

"The internal waveform monitors are now calibrated," KARR announced in its depthless mechanical buzz. *"You will now commence cleaning and realigning the power boosters."*

With a sigh she started to replace the panel, and then realized that the tip of her screwdriver was within millimeters of one of the logic banks. It might be possible to mess them up, or short them out, just by stabbing the panel. The move would not deactivate KARR, but it would eliminate all memory the machine had. It would become like a small child, not motionless, but at least helpless, and perhaps less harmful. Plus, Tony would not be able to use it to commit more mayhem. She could easily lie about a blown circuit.

She balanced the loose panel in her hand and began to probe inward with the screwdriver. No one could see her from the angle at which she was hanging out of the car.

Before the screwdriver blade was even close to the first honeycomb of logic banks, a hot jolt of electrical current raced through the panel in her hand, sparking and sizzling. With a yelp she dropped the panel and screwdriver to the floor mats. The rank smell of ozone permeated the air. At first she thought she'd blundered, but then KARR's voice addressed her.

"You are advised not to attempt to sabotage me," it said, the very even tone of its voice a threat. *"I shall increase the charge in amperage and cause extreme cellular damage if there is another such attempt."*

Bonnie had fallen from the car, and sat on the filthy floor of the Kenilworth tenement rubbing her injured hand.

"Better pay attention, babe," said a voice from behind her. It was the unctuous Tony, wearing his usual smirk. It was like an earthquake fault, cracking his face and making it ugly. "KARR means business."

Roughly, he grabbed the collar of her jumper and hauled her to her feet. She wobbled.

"Get your hands off of me, you creep!"

"Hey!" Tony said, his brow furrowing into anger and his **hand** automatically cocking back to strike her again. When she flinched, he grinned. "Be friendly, lover, or I'll scatter your teeth all over the room."

When his hand drifted down to the zipper of her coverall, she slapped it away. He merely laughed again.

"Feisty, feisty," he said. From a nearby table, he picked up a cold fryburger wrapped in greasy waxed paper and took a sloppy, wet chomp. The burger squished when he bit into it. Orange dressing squirted onto his coatfront. Tony chewed with his mouth open, his voice muffled by the too-big bite he had taken. "How about some food, babe?"

Bonnie's gorge rose. "No thanks. Not even Michael Knight would eat that garbage."

"And who the hell is Michael Knight?" Tony asked with a gross leer from behind another mouthful of sludge. "Your boyfriend?"

"When you find out, you'll wish you never asked," she said. "But you'll have lots of time to think about it in jail."

"KARR's allergic to the slammer," said Tony. "So we've decided to bypass it." He hauled an enormous wad of twenty-dollar bills from his pants and riffled through it for her benefit. "We can afford other stuff now. So you just get back to work, and after KARR's fixed up, you don't have to be bothered with us again." His face hardened. "Give us any trouble, and *you'll* wish your parents had never met. You reading me, sweetheart?"

Bonnie said nothing, but bent to pick up

the fallen screwdriver. KARR was monitoring her constantly. Tony's eyes gobbled her up lasciviously. She couldn't make a move.

Right at the moment, she would have liked to see that arrogant, self-centered egomaniac Michael Knight more than anything in the world.

She bent back inside of the cockpit of the car again. "KARR? I'd like to save the power-booster adjustments for last. Let me correct the Beta circuit for now. It'll be easier and faster if I do the circuits in order."

"*A logical progression,*" said KARR. "*You have permission to proceed.*"

Bonnie knew that KARR's power boosters—unlike the similar components in KITT she had moved to make room for the resonating laser—were malfunctioning, throwing off interference that KITT could read if he and Michael were close enough. It was like a homing beam, and she wanted to keep it going as a signal for as long as possible.

In the background, Tony flopped down into a chair, ravenously ingesting his disgusting meal and toying with his revolver. Suddenly a shot issued from behind Bonnie—a hollow boom that scared the starch out of her and echoed inside the huge, derelict lobby. For a terrified second she thought the slug had been meant for her—a cowardly shot in the back—but instead she heard something made out of glass burst apart with a crash.

Tony sat there with his simian grin, blowing smoke from the nose of the gun like Hopalong Cassidy. "Don't get so jumpy, babe," he mocked. "Just a little bit of target practice."

Several dry liquor bottles were lined up on the old registration desk across the room. The middle one had been picked off. Tony, Bonnie observed, was a pretty dead-on shot.

"I can't concentrate on this work if you're going to play shooting gallery," she said.

"Then maybe we could play instead of work," Tony suggested, his eyes lighting up and giving her another once-over.

"Do you want KARR fixed or not?"

"Okay, babe, don't get all steamed. No more shooting." He held the gun up between his thumb and forefinger for her to see and then pointedly reloaded the single spent chamber. "That is, unless you're uncooperative."

Bonnie pushed the images *that* brought up out of her head. How much longer could this ordeal last? Where the devil was Michael? What were they all doing at the foundation— had they forgotten her?

"What in God's sweet name is all the racket about?" came a different voice.

Rev lumbered across the room, scratching, still clutching a mostly empty bottle. Bonnie spotted him and remembered the description given by the Knight Industries guard who had been knocked out.

"You hafta play with that damned thing all the time?" Rev chastised Tony. "You're gonna blow your own foot off if you're not—" He stopped cold when he spotted Bonnie sticking out of the car. She withdrew and stood up to face them both, uncertain of what was happening.

Rev looked from Bonnie to Tony and back. "Have you been spending that money on fallen women, boy?" he said to Tony in a righteous tone. "You know what the Bible says about consorting with women of ill repute!"

"No, Rev, that's not—"

"Shameful, shameful." Rev clucked his tongue between slurps from the whiskey bottle.

"She's here to work on KARR," Tony said. "Fix him up so we can go on to our reward."

"Huh? Oh." The message gradually cleared through Rev's alcohol-soaked brain. "So who's the pretty lady?" He staggered toward Bonnie and looked her slowly up and down, grunting affirmation to himself. "So, young lady. Did Tony pay you a fair price for this service you are rendering us?" Confidentially he added, "He can afford it, you know."

Bonnie had to hide a smile of amusement at the crazed old apparition that had weaved up before her. "You might say I was brought here under duress," she said.

Rev's eyes widened, and he turned and heaved the liquor bottle toward Tony on the couch. Tony ducked and the bottle went off like a grenade behind him.

"Dammit, Tony, I said no kidnapping!" Rev thundered. "You lied to me and went ahead and did it anyway, didn't you, boy! I got two outstanding warrants on me already and you gotta go kidnap a mechanic! They'll lock us up and throw away the key! How do you expect to get to heaven if you lie? You gonna *lie* your way through the Pearly Gates? You involve an innocent child like this in this cesspool of criminal vice and corruption? No!"

For a moment Tony could actually believe that Rev had once been a tent-revival preacher. His voice boomed and filled up the room.

But he ran out of backbone quickly, muttering, "And damn it all to hell and brimstone, you made me break a perfectly good bottle of Ryder Dickson's finest."

Bonnie said, "I didn't want to come here. He forced me. Help me—please?"

Rev was turning when Tony's voice arrested him from across the room. "Get over here, now!" He had a newspaper in one hand, a fresh bottle in the other.

Rev went, in the manner of an iron filing attracted to a magnet, and Bonnie's flash of hope withered.

"And you." Tony stabbed a finger a her. "Finish up *now!*" She retreated back into the depths of KARR's wires and circuitry.

Rev was still angry, but Tony knew how to calm him down. He accepted the bottle that was shoved into his hand. Tony wrapped a fraternal arm around Rev's shoulder. "She's just here to fix the car, Rev. We still ain't done too much that's outside the law. And once KARR is all tuned up, why, we got us one more job in a couple of hours, and then it's all just like I said before. I wasn't lying to you."

Rev took a swig and mulled this over.

"Right here," said Tony, unfolding the newspaper onto the table across the room. "This is the big one."

Bonnie spotted them but was too far away to hear. Thinking quickly, she said, "KARR? Initiate your number-two video screen, please."

"For what purpose?"

"I want to double-check the zoom and focus," she said, having prepared a lie in case the car got nosy.

"As you wish."

The screen flared to snowy life and Bonnie adjusted several knobs, zeroing in on the paper Tony was holding. There was a two-column picture of the Ruthroff Fine Arts Museum, and a circled article whose headline read GEMS FOR MUSEUM EXHIBITION ARRIVE TODAY.

Inches from her hand was a panel that could put her in instant touch with Knight Industires, so she could warn everyone. But if she tried to signal, KARR would fry her and not a peep would get through. The machine was crafty and ruthless.

Grimly, she kept on working.

13

"I'm aware that this is a long shot, Michael,"
KITT said, "But following a long shot seems
more productive than doing nothing."

"Yeah. We were doing a lot of nothing back
at the foundation, as far as I can see."

KITT's sleek projectile shape nosed off the
freeway and grabbed an off-ramp near down-
town Los Angeles. The information they had
gathered was not substantial, but they were
acting on what they had: KITT's computer
projection of KARR's escape route, figuring
in diversionary tactics, and the computer re-
cords on Tony Coscarelli and the ex-Reverend
Jeremiah Beaudine, alias Tony Cox and Jimmy
Binder, alias Tony Cosco and Jerry Bean, alias
. . . the lists in the police files had gone on for
two full pages, listing offenses and outstand-

ing warrants for each phony name. Nobody, as it turned out, knew what the two men's real names actually were. Not that it mattered. But Michael had the lucid description given by the hospitalized guard of Rev, and the police sketch of Tony. He had expected the police computers to yield up nothing, but KITT had faithfully logged what information there was to be had—including the most likely approximation of where to look for the seedy pair.

KITT had also picked up an occasional trace reading from KARR while on the freeway. The evidence might have been a series of tantalizing, misleading carrots, to throw them off scent, but they came regularly enough to generate some hope. Now they were diverting down into the Towndale district, a clot of factories and unattractive industrial services buildings.

"What is the major product of this district?" said KITT.

Michael laughed. "Air pollution, I think."

"Michael?"

"Yes?"

"Whatever possessed you to jump onto the hood of a speeding car that had no clear intention of stopping, and every cause to do you bodily harm in furtherance of an escape which— according to KARR, at least—had to be made?"

Michael was embarrassed. "Don't ask me, KITT; I just *did* it. It always works in the movies."

"*The tone of your voice indicates otherwise. You're worried about Bonnie, aren't you?*"

"Yeah, buddy. I keep seeing her inside of KARR, struggling with the goon behind the wheel ... and there was nothing any of us could do about it." His hands flexed on KITT's wheel.

"*I, too, am concerned for Bonnie's safety,*" said KITT. "*But consider the following logical progression. It may ease your mind.*"

"Shoot," said Michael, stopping for a traffic light.

"*The choice of Bonnie for an abduction victim and the seeking out of the foundation office by KARR and his companions cannot be considered random,*" explained KITT. "*Therefore, two questions: Why the exposure to risk and capture when it would be easier to hide out, and why kidnap Bonnie?*"

"KARR needs work," Michael put in.

"*Precisely. If KARR is undergoing the type of maintenance problems only a cybernetic technician can solve, the choice of Bonnie becomes not only logical, but her abilities become her greatest asset—and they would not do harm to the only person who could help them. Additionally, Bonnie knows enough about the workings of the Knight series to signal us if she gets the chance, using KARR'S own emissions. She is also resourceful enough to find another way to contact us if she is held long enough—so, the longer she's there, the greater our chances of saving her and capturing KARR and the criminals at the same time."*

"You're right, KITT, except for one thing."

"I'm listening."

"I don't think Bonnie's the type to blithely cooperate with guys who would just grab her and start giving orders, you know what I mean?"

"Bonnie does tend to be headstrong and contrary," said KITT.

Especially around me, Michael thought, but KITT was right. The implacable logic of the machine. "They might have to force her to repair KARR," he said. "There are a lot of ways to coerce people without killing them outright . . . although the ways often make you wish you were dead." He had flashed back to his unpleasant experiences as a prisoner of war in Vietnam. Oh yeah, we have ways of making you sing like a canary, he thought. "She might refuse outright, figuring we're going to show up and save her. Remember that Tony guy has a gun, now. If she tells them no and remains immovable, all we might find is a dead body."

"You have quite a pessimistic way of looking at events," said KITT.

"Chalk it up to experience."

"But you're right, of course. You seem to understand the logic of illogic better than anyone I know."

Michael did not ask KITT what *that* meant, but it brought a brief smile to his lips . . .

which vanished when he thought of the pickle Bonnie might be in.

"You've realized by now that Bonnie's special abilities have caused another problem," added KITT.

They were cruising Towndale's side streets now, crawling up one and down another. "I hope you're scanning as well as talking," Michael said.

"Of course. Picking up nothing significant yet. The factory complexes surrounding us are not the best atmosphere in which to pick out KARR's interference."

"So what's the problem?"

"Bonnie is the only person who can tune and calibrate the laser. It cannot be fired until it is properly calibrated. . . ."

"Nobody told me anything about tuning the laser!" said Michael. "I thought it was installed and ready to go!"

"Yes to the former, but no to the latter, I'm afraid."

"What about Devon? Can't he do it?"

"There are a number of technicians at the Knight estate facility that could do it," noted KITT. *"But to do that in Los Angeles without Bonnie, we'd have to contact an independent technician, who—"*

"I get it," said Michael. "We don't have the time, and you're supposed to be a secret, and so on." Although the technology built into KITT wasn't going to be very secret for much longer if KARR continued its spree of destruction and thwarting the cops.

"Until further developments," said KITT, "I'll assume that we'll find Bonnie in time, and that calibration of the laser will be the least of our worries."

Michael turned down another side street. "That's it, KITT. Be positive, be positive."

The monitors jumped and registered various kinds of stray power outputs, but nothing that fit KARR's peculiar configuration.

"You sure there's no way to fire the laser?" said Michael. "Not even blind?"

"The best qualified person to do that would be—"

"Bonnie. Right. I read you."

"That damned car has changed you, Tony," Rev was saying. He shook his head as though Tony's fate was corrupt and predetermined.

"Look, will you *forget* the holy-roller stuff and pay attention?" He brandished the folded newspaper advertising the forthcoming gem exhibition. "We pull off this job and we can be shut of this dump, and the car, and the girl, so there's no problem."

Rev was not listening, nor did he appear interested anymore in the job that could put him and Tony on their fantasized Easy Street for the rest of their lives. He was ignoring his bottle now, his red-rimmed eyes suspicious and his voice sunk in pronouncements of doom. "Tony, are you familiar with what Lucifer did up in heaven—before he was caused to fall?"

"Rev, knock it off!"

"He built a machine—the Bible says so, an infernal machine!"

They had Bonnie's attention again. She stopped working on KARR and looked over the door panel. If she could clearly hear their argument from across the vast lobby, she figured that KARR was picking it up, too.

"Sounds like your partners aren't too loyal, KARR," she said, attempting to stir up the soup a bit. Maybe it would provide her with an opportunity for escape.

"Mr. Tony and Mr. Rev are my benefactors. Their disagreement is personal and therefore, irrelevant."

"You just keep thinking that," she said, mentally adding *you metal moron.* "That way, when they finally turn on you you'll never even feel the time lag between their betrayal and the scrap heap."

The car did not respond.

Rev pushed away from Tony's attempt at a calming embrace. "It's an infernal machine, and we've got to stop it before it's too late, and we're damned for all eternity!"

Tony accepted the rebuff. He knew what was happening now. When Rev got really lubricated, he would occasionally fly off on wild binges of Bible symbology and religious ranting and raving, like a TV evangelist with a snake in one hand and a collection plate in the other. The fact that this had not recurred recently was a testament to the lousy and low-grade booze Rev had been imbibing over the last three or four months. But now, with a day's backlog of classier liquor fizzing away in his bloodstream, the stump-revival preacher of Rev's distant past came surging forth with werewolf swiftness and intensity.

He was waving his arms wildly. "The police will know what to do with KARR! It's not for us to tamper with anymore!"

Tony grabbed Rev's coat sleeve briskly. "Yo, yo . . . what's all this about the police—?"

"Hear that?" whispered Bonnie to KARR. "They're going to turn you over, and you know what that means? The slammer, KARR. The pokey. The end."

"You will complete the adjustment of the Lambda circuit immediately or you shall receive an increased charge," the machine said flatly.

Bonnie smiled and continued tinkering. She was getting KARR's goat.

Tony held Rev at the end of his arm and glared at him. He understood perfectly what was going on, but that did not prevent him from thinking that perhaps the whole plan would run a bit smoother if Rev was out of the picture. It would be so much easier to put Rev's lights out and leave him for the cops— since he wanted to see the cops so bad anyway—and then have a few laughs with the brunette cookie, and then dump her somewhere. After that it would just be him and KARR, with nothing to stop them. If snatching the babe had been accomplished so easily, getting more hydrogen fuel should be no problem. . . . Sure, he thought. Why not?

"Adjustment completed," Bonnie said, screwing the hatch lid back into place. At the same time she gauged the distance from her current position to the front door. She was an able sprinter—one hundred yards in 13.4 seconds, on the track and wearing a jogging suit—and KARR was conveniently pointed the wrong way. All that needed to happen was for the argument between Tony and Rev to heat up just enough for them to ignore her for . . . five seconds, she decided. Tony's reaction time with the gun would eat up another second; two, if she lucked out. Maybe Rev would oblige by getting in the way?

"Let go of me, Tony!" Rev bellowed. "This is for our own good!" He tried to break out of Tony's grip but was unsuccessful.

"Like hell!" yelled Tony into his face, growing florid. "You're forgetting about a lot of stuff! You're hiding behind that holier-than-thou crap because you're afraid to make the big score! You wanna live in the gutter all your life, you poor, screwed-up slob?" He was shaking Rev now, and the older man lolled. "You know how much money you're gonna lose us by fooling around?"

"I don't care about the money," Rev wailed.

"I care about your immortal soul!" He jerked hard and slipped free of Tony's grip.

It was clear he was leaving, and in that second Tony acted.

His hand caught the half-empty liquor bottle in Rev's. He brought it up quickly and shattered it across Rev's forehead. Whiskey soaked into Rev's white hair and, after he collapsed to the floor and stopped moving, began to mix with fresh blood.

"Sorry, Rev," he said. "Give my regards to Jesus." A sudden noise snapped Tony's head around.

He turned just in time to see Bonnie's white jumper vanish around the corner leading to the hotel's old front doors.

The pistol was out in an instant, but it was an instant too late. He cocked the hammer and ran across the room.

"KARR! Why the hell didn't you stop her?" he shouted angrily, as he passed the parked vehicle.

"I was noting your deactivation of Mr. Rev. Did he seek to return me to the slammer?"

"Yeah, yeah—look, KARR, we gotta stop that girl, or she's gonna do the same thing Rev was planning behind our backs!"

"She leaped away before I could apply a charge. I am not the right size to give chase through the front hallway. I assumed you would have instructions regarding her apprehension?"

"Right! Let's go. She can't get far on foot," Tony realized, wiping his mouth nervously.

"I know this neighborhood. And if I can't pick her off from the car ..." His wolfish grin reappeared and he jumped into KARR's cockpit. "Then we'll just mow her down! Let's go!"

Bonnie made sure she didn't look back when she lit out for the door. She simply ran as fast as her body could move her, cursing the exercise time she had sacrificed recently in order to keep KITT in running condition.

She rounded the corner wildly, grabbing the ornamental molding for stability, and headed for the front door. When she heard Tony shouting in the background, she quickly opened the door and slammed it, stepping back into the shadows of an alcove in the hallway rather than fleeing outside.

Apparently, her ruse succeeded—and she heard KARR fire up and Tony had not come running into the hallway after her. They'd waste a good five minutes looking around for her outside and all she had to do was hang tight and stay hidden. She wished the place had had a functioning telephone, but that was a pipe dream.

Now if only Michael Knight could figure out where the devil she was. . . .

14

"Getting some activity on the scanner, Michael," said KITT. *"The configurations conform to KARR's."*

Michael suddenly found himself paying quite a lot of attention. "Which way?"

"Southeast. One-point-five miles."

A pinpoint light blinked over the street map displayed on one of KITT's video screens. As Michael watched, the light shifted. KARR was on the move.

He grabbed a nearby corner, then another, speeding up to cut time. Bonnie was being held captive somewhere in the vicinity.

"Catch anything now?" he said.

"Strong emissions, definitely from KARR's power booster," replied KITT. *"Eighty degrees southeast of us now."*

Michael smacked the steering wheel. "Where *are* they? We should be right on top of them. . . ."

"*Correction. The blip has stopped moving. I can't tell now whether it's KARR or my own sensor echo.*"

"Didn't they do this in an old submarine movie?" said Michael. "Don't waste any time. We'll triangulate. Make two more circuits of this six-block area, the one on the screen, and we'll pinpoint from that."

A display of the triangulation appeared on the second video monitor, outlined in yellow.

"*It's still not moving,*" said KITT unnecessarily. "*If it's KARR, it's parked dead still.*"

"Setting up an ambush, maybe."

"*Possible, Michael. One circuit completed.*"

"Can KARR detect you the same way you can find him?"

"*Also possible, but I lack sufficient data to say one way or the other. I estimate that my own emissions are unique, and therefore present a 'signature' to the correct detection apparatus. Whether KARR is capable of making this distinction with his sub-par equipment, I cannot say.*"

"You're bragging, KITT. Setting yourself up as better than KARR because you hate the idea you're not one of a kind." Michael was amused.

"*Not at all, Michael,*" KITT objected prissily. "*My equipment is superior.*"

"Including your driver?"

KITT had no comment to offer on that and instead told Michael that the second circuit was finished and the triangulation complete. KARR—or whatever appeared to the scanners as KARR—was three blocks away from their current position.

"Okay, KITT," said Michael. "I want you to shut your engine down and run in on battery power, just in case KARR's ears are working."

"A surprise attack?" said KITT.

"You got it. Let's go."

After making a fast, fishtailing circuit of the Kenilworth building and not spotting Bonnie—that white jumper of hers not only outlined her curves, Tony thought, but it made her a sitting duck in the twilight since everything else in Towndale seemed dead gray— Tony slammed on the brakes and stopped in front of the boarded-up entrance to the old hotel.

"Maybe she pulled a fast one on us," he said to KARR. "Maybe she's still hiding out inside."

"I register a body-heat reading," KARR said. *"With rapid and shallow respirations. A different reading from that of the nonfunctional Mr. Rev."*

"That must be her—panting from the chase," said Tony. "Wait right here."

He opened the driver's door and withdrew

the revolver. Walking in a careful stalking motion toward the boards over the entrance—formerly an imposing set of brass-handled double doors—he peered between two of the planks.

Huddled inside, Bonnie saw the searching eyes and froze. She did not think she could be seen. The shadows in the entrance alcove were pretty impenetrable.

She looked up and saw the muzzle of the pistol poke between the boards.

Bonnie dived just as a shot exploded in the alcove, blowing a ragged hole in the plaster inches from where her head had been. She flattened onto the floor as lath and dust fell on top of her, and then pushed off, running back the way she had come. Outside, she could hear Tony's taunting and victorious voice.

"Flushed ya out, baby!" he was yelling. "Just like a sewer rat stuck in a drainpipe!

Tony kicked the boards down and gave chase, a maniac smile plastered across his face.

Bonnie vaulted over Rev's prostrate form and ran for the hallway leading—she hoped—to an alternate exit. Another hot slug whizzed past her face and plowed into the wall.

"Come to Papa!" Tony shouted after her.

She found a stairway and took the steps three at a time going up. The second floor was abandoned, windblown, and creaky—apparently one of the reasons the Kenilworth had been condemned nearly two decades ago. She tried to tread softly, to keep the boards from squeaking, but already she heard Tony galloping up the stairs behind her.

He appeared in the archway and fired off two more rounds into opposite corners of the room to cause her to betray her position again. This time she flinched but held, hiding behind a delapidated cocktail bar in what seemed to be a derelict upstairs lounge.

He has one more shot left, she thought. No, two. This was a hell of a time to get confused and forget her math.

Another report shook the rafters, and a bullet punched a splintery passageway through the top of the bar and ricocheted away.

Tony cursed and ducked back out the door, checking the upstairs hallway. As he did so Bonnie moved to a window. She was considering the stomach-wrenching possibility of jumping down from the second floor to escape.

Outside she saw a silent black shape cruising slowly up the street to the rear of the hotel. Assuming this was KARR, she kept quiet.

Below, neither Michael nor KITT detected the stained white jumper poking out of the second-floor window.

"Freeze it solid right there, babe," came Tony's reptilian voice from the doorway.

She was caught.

"Don't jump. You're too high up and you'll

break your pretty neck—and I'm not finished with you yet."

She almost jumped out the window—almost. Tony cut loose a shot into the ceiling to dissuade her, and what happened next happened too fast to perceive with leisure.

All she saw was an enormous ceiling beam crashing down, unhinged by the loud vibrations of the gunshot, and by the bullet itself, hammering into the weakened ceiling. It swung down between them like a huge ax, cleaving a yawning hole in the floor and raising choking clouds of dust and broken plasterboard. Tony was shielding his eyes. Bonnie felt the entire floor shift, as if it planned to join the ground floor any moment.

Outside, KITT finally registered the gunshots and commotion, just as he was about to make the turn that would have revealed KARR sitting parked in front of the Kenilworth. Instead, Michael shouted, "KITT! Get us in there, and fast!"

KITT complied. He used up the remaining half block to accelerate, then hung a sharp ninety-degree turn right into the brick wall of the hotel.

Bricks and wallboard coughed inward in a shower just as the heavy beam took out a portion of the ceiling above. Michael keyed his window quickly down.

Bonnie's head jerked around when she heard Michael calling her name. "Michael!" she yelled. "I'm up—"

205 TRUST DOESN'T RUST

"Hey, Michael!" Tony drowned her out. "I got your chick up here, so no funny business or she gets filled full of holes!"

Bonnie heard the sound of tinkling brass amid the other cascading junk and saw that Tony had expertly jacked out his spent shells and replaced them already with one of the speed-load rings stolen from the guard at the Knight labs. Once again, he had a full six shots; the hammer was back and the barrel aimed at her midsection. He was too close to miss.

Michael quickly flipped on KITT's amplifier and loudspeaker. "Don't hurt her and you can go free!" he said, hating it.

"I don't believe you!" Tony answered. "No deal!" Then, in as loud a voice as possible, he added, "KARR! If you can hear me, get in here now!"

All of them paused in anticipation of KARR's entrance. For a few seconds there was no sound whatsoever.

Then Tony's face put on its lopsided grin as the distant turbine whine got louder.

The whole Kenilworth building rattled violently when KARR cleared away the front entrance where Bonnie had concealed herself—the alcove, most of the hallway—and burst forth into the lobby behind a spray of demolished concrete and trashed chandeliers, wallboard, carpeting, and steel. Doors with broken backs flew across the room; billows of smoky dust-fog kicked up and obscured everything. The Kenilworth seemed to rock; the collapse of the entire structure seemed imminent.

Tony backed toward the stairs. "Now we'll say good-bye," he said. "Till later."

Then he squeezed off two shots at Bonnie.

She knew he was going to try to kill her. Even across the floating dust clouds, she saw the glint of death in his eye, and as he squeezed the trigger she did the only thing she thought was possible under the circumstances.

She dived flat-out through the ragged hole in the floor.

Her outstretched hand caught an iron reinforcing rod on the way through, and it absorbed the shock of her dive, savaging her shoulder muscles as her grip impelled her into a clumsy backward somersault. Her weight defeated the grip, her hand jerked loose, and she fell toward the lobby floor like a skydiver.

She landed with a brutal *thump* on top of KITT, scaring the dickens out of Michael before she rolled to the side. He recognized her as she sprawled onto the floor in a scatter of arms and legs.

KITT automatically sprang the passenger door open. Bonnie shook her head to condense the mutiple images her eyes were sending in, and, still sitting awkwardly on the floor, squinted myopically at the occupant of the black car.

"Michael?" she said, stunned and disbelieving.

"Get in!" he shouted, motioning furiously for her to hurry up.

On the other side of the room, Tony tore down the stairs and ran for KARR's waiting door. Once behind it, he paused to snap off two more shots in KITT's direction to buy time.

The light Special police slugs scratched off KITT's windshield, leaving firy yellow trails.

Bonnie scrambled into the car and slammed the door. Breathlessly, she asked, "What took you so long?"

"Traffic was murder," said Michael.

Tony got his door closed simultaneously with Bonnie, and for a heart-stopping second the two supercars faced each other across the Kenilworth's lobby. Then KARR revved his engine, preparing for escape.

"The detritus of the unsound structure behind us prevents going out the way I entered," said KARR to Tony. *"Brace for turbo-boost."*

"Yeah!" said Tony, red and sweating. "Go!"

"KITT!" said Michael. "Cut him off!"

"I can't, Michael," responded the machine. *"I will cause harm to the unconscious man on the floor if I move to block KARR."*

That was all they had time for.

KARR rocketed forward, picking up speed at an amazing rate, bursting apart the arrangement of seats in the middle of the room.

Chairs flew like ninepins. There was a thunderclap of compression, and inches before the front wheels could crush Rev's skull, they left the ground as KARR took to the air. The turbo-booster thrust lifted the vehicle over KITT to land with a building-jolting crash of impact on the far side.

"Back into him, KITT, now!" Michael ordered.

"He's going too fast!" Bonnie said.

She was right. Before they could muster the speed to cause any kind of effective collision, KARR dug its own tunnel through yet another of the Kenilworth building's remaining walls. Timbers and tons of structural fall-out rained down in its wake.

Then there came a deeper creaking, more ominous and more fundamental.

Michael and Bonnie both glanced toward the ceiling just as it caved in.

KITT roared forward, and for a moment it seemed the car had gone as crazy as its criminal opposite number and was trying to run down the still-unconscious Rev. But KITT braked before impact, his nose within a hair of Rev's prone form.

Then the ceiling—and most of the building, weakened by the loud noises and by having so many of its walls kicked out in so short a time—folded inward to meet them. Bricks and rubble showered down and began to pile up, burying the black car in an impromptu tomb.

Debris continued to pile up until KITT was no longer visible.

The Kenilworth building had ceased to exist, and all that was left was floating dust and silence.

15

"Relax, Michael, will you?" came Bonnie's voice. It was muffled, because at the first sign of the ceiling yielding to gravity, Michael had automatically yanked her head down and shielded her with his own arms and shoulders.

He looked up, feeling foolish. What was left of the building was piled up all around KITT, blocking the windows and plunging the interior of the car into darkness. It was entirely immobilized, but undamaged.

"Sorry," said Michael, sitting up and releasing her. "KITT, why the devil didn't you just drive us out of this mess?"

"The man on the floor would have been crushed and suffocated," explained the car, calmly. *"As it is, the debris is piled up against my hood—and not on the man."*

"That's Rev," said Bonnie. "At least that's what the other guy called him. I think he needs an ambulance, and right now. His so-called partner opened up his head with a whiskey bottle. Nasty."

"KITT, get ahold of Devon and tell him to send a para-medic unit." Looking around at the garbage that entombed them, he added ruefully, "And a couple of tow trucks—or maybe a bulldozer. Can you move at all?"

The engine whirred strenuously, to no effect. *"Negative. I'm afraid I need some elbow room in order to work up the momentum to burst out."*

"That's just wonderful," Michael said. "And where's our friend off to?"

"He's planning to rip off the gem show at the Ruthroff Museum," said Bonnie. "His partner wouldn't go along with him."

"That means we just . . . sit here and do nothing until Devon calls in some reinforcements." Michael was fuming at being trapped and outfoxed purely by random chance and ancient building construction.

"Well," Bonnie said, notching the passenger seatback so she could relax. "Thanks for coming to my rescue anyway." She brushed hair out of her eyes and smiled. "I'm exhausted. Might as well catnap or something until we're disinterred. And thanks for throwing yourself over me—what a chivalrous thing to do."

Michael calmed down a bit. "Yeah."

"Provided you weren't just making a pass at me," Bonnie put in.

Michael blushed. "I assure you as a co-worker in the great Knight Industries mega-monolith, madam, that my intentions are strictly honorable."

She settled back and closed her eyes. "Darn."

"Michael? Bonnie? Please tell me what's going on," came Devon's voice over the speaker.

Michael sat bolt upright. "Devon, down in Towndale someplace a building just caved in. We're underneath it. You've got to get us out—KITT can't budge, not even with turbo-boost. And get an ambulance down here, pronto. Warn the police that KARR is on its way to the Ruthroff—wait a minute." He turned to Bonnie. "Where are they safekeeping the gems? The museum or the warehouse?"

"The newspaper mentioned the warehouse," remembered Bonnie.

"The warehouse, Devon. I don't know if there's enough time to do anything about it, but that's the plan. We're stuck here."

"Why the ambulance?" said Devon. "Which of you is hurt?"

"Our first suspect, the one from the night of the Knight labs rip-off, is underneath KITT. KITT kept him from being squashed while KARR nearly flattened him. Bonnie says he's alive but I don't know whether he's too seriously hurt to last. You read me?"

"Units are on their way. Meet me at the

Ruthroff warehouse as soon as you're mobile. It could take about fifteen minutes."

"With something like KARR, I could steal a couple million bucks in fifteen minutes," muttered Michael, the memory of the previous night's bank jobs fresh in his mind. "Just hurry," he ended.

"*I am sorry, Michael, for fouling your plan up,*" said KITT. "*Seeing that other car, and knowing its potential for harm and destruction—*"

"Yeah, I know, KITT. It shakes me up, too."

The digital clock on the dashboard became an instrument of torture as Michael endured unending minutes waiting for someone else to come pull his fat out of the fire. He glanced over at Bonnie and saw that her lashes were down and her breathing was steady and slight. Safe inside of KITT, she had promptly dropped off to sleep.

He shifted in his seat so he could study her face. There did not seem to be any better way to kill the time.

After endless reassurances over the radio, followed by the rumble of unseen heavy equipment, the avalanche of junk blocking KITT's rear window fell away. KITT shifted into his automatic mode and backed out.

Bonnie came awake, eyes bleary. Surrounding the car were workmen, police, and paramedics.

And Michael was still there, to her left.

"You need any kind of medical attention?" he said, impatient to hit the road and catch up with KARR.

"Wait a minute," she said, getting out of the car.

Rev was still in front of KITT, curled up on the floor—snoring. A young man with an Emergency Medical Technician patch on the shoulder of his blue shirt knelt and recorded the old man's vital signs after tending to the cuts on his head.

He looked up to see Bonnie peering past him. "He'll pull through, ma'am," he said. "Old dude's got a pretty hard head. It looks nastier than it is. Mostly, I'd say he's sleeping off a hell of a binge. You know him?"

"Yeah," she said. "I think he helped save my life."

"Bonnie!"

At Michael's urgent call she turned and got back into the car. The other officials in attendance knew better than to waste time now with protocol; they were aware of Michael's mission and got out of his way.

After they maneuvered around the wreckage of the Kenilworth and regained access to the (gloriously fat and unobstructed, Michael thought) street, Bonnie said, "I suppose the blow on the head and the amount of alcohol combined to put Rev under. You did the right thing, KITT—if you hadn't intervened, he surely would have been killed."

"My calculations seemed to indicate the liklihood. Thank you, Bonnie."

"If you're going to dive, you shouldn't drink," said Michael, waiting for a reaction. "Get it?"

"No comment," said Bonnie.

"Your sense of humor continues to go beyond my capacity for comprehension, Michael," KITT added.

"Well, here's something that isn't so funny," Michael went on. "Saving that old guy's life got us trapped, and probably put the gems at the Ruthoff Museum warehouse in jeopardy. We can still lose KARR, you know."

His pronouncement sobered the group, and they drove in silence for a few miles until Devon's voice came over the speakers again.

"Michael? I'm still en route to the warehouse, but the transmissions on the police band indicate trouble." At least Devon wasn't freaking out; his voice was cool and even.

"Great," Michael complained. "We're still ten miles away and hitting traffic."

"Do the best you can. You may have to pursue KARR beyond the warehouse."

"I sort of expected that." He pushed KITT's speed up another fifteen miles and began to bob and weave around the cars ahead. Angry motorists honked. "Bonnie, the joystick control for the laser is on the floor in the back. Can you do anything about calibrating the laser while we're en route?"

Bonnie craned around to lift the box. It was featureless gray metal, with a LED digital readout panel and a targeting joystick. "No. I'd have to get under the hood again, and that would take time." She let Michael hang for a beat, then added, "However, I can fire the laser manually with this, provided you can aim the car, since the targeting device isn't connected to KITT's computer yet."

"Blind shot?"

"No, more like as much precision as we can manage on the run. We'll definitely have to get closer than planned."

"KITT, can you hold a head-on charge steady enough to allow Bonnie to fire? And maintain it for two seconds?"

"I notice that you haven't included time to swerve out of the way after Bonnie makes her shot," said KITT.

"Can you do it or not?"

"I'll try as hard as both of you are prepared to," the car responded.

"All for one and one for all," said Michael. "If we don't all die together, then we'll all die separate—"

"Can we change the subject?" Bonnie interrupted.

"Work in the field getting too much for you?" Michael ran KITT up too close behind a lumbering semi and whipped past it in the breakdown lane. Behind them the truck's air horn went off deafeningly and the driver shook his fist out the window at the nut in the black car.

"After this little adventure I'm perfectly content to stay on the research end," Bonnie said. She knew what Michael was getting at but decided not to take his bait. She'd lambasted him earlier for treating KITT—and by extension, her work—roughly in "the field," and it was true that she had not fully appreciated the kind of risks Michael took on as a matter of course. But Michael Knight was about to find out that his disdain for her scientific talents—too often ignored in favor of chatting her up like any other member of his seraglio— was about to get neutralized as well, in a kind of balance of justice between them. She would prove to him that she could fire an uncalibrated laser, under extreme pressure, and hit what she aimed at. Then maybe the little arguments and digs would cease, and they could perhaps progress to a more adult kind of relationship.

"Devon?" Michael was trying to key the radio again. "No answer. He must be out of the limo."

Bonnie pointed. "Grab the interchange here. Maybe we can cut some time off the drive."

They finally evaded the thicker traffic and picked up speed, zooming along the surface streets and avoiding L.A.'s infamous freeway snarls.

What they saw on arrival at the Ruthroff Museum's warehouse facility did not surprise Michael at all, but he nevertheless felt a sinking feeling in his stomach when his eyes confirmed what had taken place only moments before.

There was a KARR-sized hole in the side of the building. It looked like a hungry mouth.

Devon stood waiting for them in the middle of the entry hole KARR had hacked out of the concrete block wall. KARR's escape was obviously old news already.

Michael was out of the car in a flash, running toward Devon. "How bad?" he said, skipping the amenities.

"The guard force had been tripled, for all the good it did," said Devon. "They all fell over themselves getting out of KARR's way once the wall was penetrated. Inside the warehouse was worse—men shooting wildly, and to no effect. They finally realized that in surrounding the car they were shooting at each other, that the bullets had no effect on KARR anyway, and that ricocheting shells were damaging some of the valuable artworks kept in the warehouse." Devon shrugged; the expression was one of disgust at waste. "For safekeeping."

"Sounds like a real Keystone Kops scene," said Michael, stepping through the hole and catching sight of the black, looping tire marks all over the concrete floor.

"KARR herded the inside guards into a corner and trapped them there with a huge packing crate. It was absurd. No doubt the scanners told the driver where the gems were—"

"And he went right to them, I'll bet," said

Michael. "Like a police dog sniffing out a heroin stash."

"The jewels were labeled, crated, and guarded inside the warehouse vault," continued Devon. He pointed toward a layered steel door, the type seen in most banks. It was lying on the floor. "Our man simply plugged the car into the safe and began loading. KARR deflected most of the shots that came his way—long enough, at least, for him to make off with four crates of gems. The stars of the gem show, I might add." Devon ticked them off on his fingers. "The Etruscan crown emerald collection. T'ang Dynasty jades. The Ghopal Singh royal standards, encrusted with rubies and gold. An entire crate of Senji Industries pearls, huge and perfect and black as midnight in a coal mine. He also got some of the newest and most spectacular M'Waba Ako diamonds." Devon stuck his hands in his pockets and appeared nervous, and that knocked Michael off balance. The KARR affair had become not only serious, but maybe fatal.

"How long ago?" said Michael. "Looks like this happened yesterday."

"Shots were fired as little as twelve minutes ago."

"At the departing car?"

"Correct. Seventeen police chase units followed it. Eight have reported back in, lost. Four haven't been heard from since they left."

"Which direction?"

Devon pointed. "Northwest, toward the coast roads."

"That's all I need, Devon," Michael said, patting him on the shoulder. "Get on the horn and I'll stay in touch." He hurried back toward KITT.

Bonnie was waiting inside, the laser joystick control balanced on one thigh while she made some minute adjustment below her side of the Super Dash.

"Readings, KITT?"

The entire area is heavy with KARR's signature radiation and emissions," reported KITT. *"Estimate of when it came through here—eleven-point-seven-five minutes ago."*

"Right on the money, KITT. He went that-away." Michael pointed toward the descending, late-afternoon sun. "And he probably left an emission trail for us to track him by all the way."

"I examined the configurations of KARR's output on the video minitor," said Bonnie. "It's rawer. The waveforms are knife-edged and asymmetrical."

Michael put KITT through a forty-five-degree turnaround and followed KARR's path out the feeder road, away from the Ruthroff warehouse. "If somebody diagnosed me like that I'd check into a hospital," he said. "What's it mean?"

"That the decay in KARR's power boosters— the thing I kept putting off repairing after I'd been abducted—is not only worse than it was five hours ago, but it's accelerating. It's getting worse geometrically, and once those power cells start bleeding energy among each other, it's time to find some good cover and shut your eyes for the big bang." She depressed a test stud on the joystick box and said. "The laser shows *ready.*"

"Having any trouble tracking KARR?" said Michael.

"To my scanners the trail is painfully evident," said KITT. *"No problem."*

Michael gave the pedal more weight, and the red neon numbers gathered themselves beyond one hundred miles an hour. He and Bonnie were pushed gently back into their seats by the speed.

Five minutes later KITT reported, *"Stronger readings coming in now, and in a discrete line."*

Bonnie glanced at one of the monitors. "Good Lord. You couldn't miss it—it's like following the vapor trail of a comet."

"Devon?" Michael said to the radio. "Can you ring up some police support to rendezvous with us about thirty miles up the coastal access road?"

"For what purpose, Michael? Surely you know a roadblock won't do any good."

"Maybe not," he said. "But Bonnie reports KARR is running out of spunk fast. They can't just keep going; they're going to have to turn and fight because they're losing options quickly. We'll need the police to help keep innocent bystanders out of the way. The coast road is loaded with scenic lookout points, and there are still a lot of tourists shooting snapshots."

As Michael spoke one such rest area blurred past on the left, crowded with Winnebagos and vehicles bearing out-of-state plates. Hewn from the cliffsides and hemmed in by low flagstone safety walls, these modest offroad stops offered spectacular views of the Pacific Ocean. As KITT caught up with the road and began to run parallel to the sea, Michael saw the sun dipping toward the horizon. A lot of people would be waiting for the sunset.

"They're on their way, Michael," said Devon. "Good luck."

"Over and out," acknowledged Michael.

"KARR must have eluded his other pursuers," said KITT.

"How do you figure?" said Michael.

"Because I read him as being somewhere inside of the next ten miles. Northward progress has stopped."

Michael and Bonnie looked at each other. Bonnie bit her lower lip.

"Then it looks like this is it," Michael said, watching the final miles clock off on the counter. "Let's go call him out."

Tony gazed absently out over the ocean.

He had shaken the last of the chase cars awhile back. They'd ceased trying to outrace KARR and cut speed, peeling off. No one had hugged his tail for ten miles. Now KARR was plugged into a parking slot at one of the scenic overlooks, mostly undetectable from the highway. Far away to one side there sat a top-heavy mobile home vehicle; an equal distance away on the opposite side there was a road-dusty Volkswagen bug.

An overweight tourist wearing a billowing aloha shirt climbed out of the back of the home/camper and lumbered toward the safety wall with his Instamatic camera. The camper lifted on its wheels when his gross weight was removed from it. The guy was fat, bald, loud, and obviously fairly well off. The picture was not Tony's idea of the good life.

He diverted his attention to the skintight cutoffs worn by the driver of the Volkswagen. She was a real California girl, Tony thought, with all that blond hair and a tan that went on forever. Now *that*, thought Tony, was the good life—that and the trunkload of jewels and cash KARR was toting for him. He had already formulated a vague plan to drive north, maybe to San Francisco, where Benny the Ritz lived. Benny could take the stones off his hands, cut them down, and fence them for twenty-five percent of the take. Benny could also help him launder the stacks of stolen cash, just in case any of the banks Tony had knocked off kept track of serial numbers. With the jewels dumped into the underground network and the cash washed—even if he only got twenty-five cents on the dollar, he'd still be pigsty-rich—Tony would be untraceable; he would cease to exist. He wanted to keep

KARR but knew the wheels would probably have to be dumped. Maybe he could drive to Vancouver, dead north. He'd never been in another country before. Yeah—ditch KARR at the border after visiting Benny the Ritz and take a day or two in San Francisco to deck out in some fancy clothes and get some matched hide suitcases for all his money, and catch a plane to Canada.

But first Tony wanted two things. Three, he thought, if you count the chick. He wanted the license plates and registration from the Volkswagen—they were currently stickered California plates and by now the cops had the details on the stolen ones KARR was wearing—and he wanted whatever was sitting around loose inside the fat man's mobile home. That he already had enough money to last three lifetimes was of no importance to his thief's mentality, and the thought of taking what he wanted—both from Fatso and the doll—at gunpoint appealed to his need for violence. He had to show everybody who was boss.

KARR sat between the other two vehicles, cooling off. At least, that's what Tony guessed the car was doing. It had beefed about some kind of leakage while they were making their getaway, and while Tony did not pretend to understand what KARR's technical explanation meant, he was sympathetic to the suggestion that they stop so KARR could quit putting out whatever it was that (it said) was making them easy to trace. Tony knew the value of throwing off a tail.

The blonde was sitting on the low stone wall, her hair wafting about in the evening breeze. Tony's eyes ravished her up and down, and he decided to clean out the fat tourist first. He felt inside his jacket for his newly reloaded gun. After throwing some slugs back at the inept guards at the Ruthroff warehouse, he was down to his last ring of bullets.

He heard the turbine whine, spun with the gun out, and at first thought KARR was taking off without him, double-crossing the double-crosser. But KARR was still parked. This was the *other* car, the one he'd outfoxed twice now.

"KARR!" he shouted, jumping into the pilot bucket. "They're back for more punishment!"

While KITT approached from the rear, KARR backed out in a spray of gravel as its tires dug for traction. It smashed solidly into KITT's oncoming front end and both cars shuddered with impact, breaking into a skidding V-formation.

KARR's wheels spun and it fishtailed madly around, so that for a moment Tony and Michael were face-to-face with less than a foot of distance separating their windows. Then Tony and KARR peeled out for the highway, Tony's tawdry little fantasies forgotten.

"How's your motor, partner?" Tony said.

"The brief rest seems to have allowed the

power-flow fluctuations to stabilize," said KARR.
*"But you realize of course that our pursuer is
probably fully fueled. In the interests of self-
preservation, and seeing that the inferior production-line version of myself refuses to give up the
chase, I would suggest elimination of the car as
soon as possible. My power-cell life at this moment is uncertain."*

"Boom him, huh? Yeah, I think you're right."
As they talked, they ate up the highway doing
one hundred and thirty. KITT was a black
shadow in the rearview mirror.

"Obstruction ahead," said KARR.

"What kind of obstruction?" said Tony, but
then he saw and recognized it.

Three armored police SWAT trucks were
blocking the roadway. On either side were
portions of the hill through which the coast
road had been carved, and there was no mar-
gin for slipping past. Perhaps twenty men
were clad in bulky flak jackets, toting M-16s
and riot guns. Tony recognized rifle grenades,
from movies he'd seen as a kid.

"They brought up the heavy artillery, pal!"
he said. "Do we just blast through the trucks?"

*"Considering conservation of my available
power,"* said KARR, *"I think turbo-boosting
over the obstruction would be more practical.
The turbo-boost is a matter of compression,
and squanders less fuel."*

"I'm all for, like, ecology," said Tony. "But
that doesn't get rid of the guy behind us.
What about him?"

"We are quite close to the ocean. Suggest ramming them from the side in order to push them over the edge so pursuit will cease."

"Great!" said Tony, stomping on the brakes and spinning KARR around to face the oncoming KITT. "We'll boom these dummies, and then leap right over the cops!"

Grabbing the wheel firmly, Tony charged KITT head-on.

They had not really expected it to be as simple as driving around a bend in the road and seeing KARR calmly parked by the seaside, and so when they did, they were unprepared. When KARR backed into them, the joystick control was jolted out of Bonnie's grasp, and she spent part of the ensuing chase fishing around on the floorboards for it. Michael had muttered something about KARR hitting the SWAT roadblock any minute, and as he hoped, KARR turned to do battle before dispensing with the police.

"Here he comes!" he said, watching KARR's headlights swelling large in front of him. "Bonnie, get ready to fire!"

Bonnie was leaned over, watching the green targeting grid imposed on KITT's video monitor. KARR showed up as a red X, getting bigger as they converged. She was able to connect the visual function to the targeting computer in the few moments they'd grabbed in transit from Kenilworth to the Ruthroff warehouse. The targeting computer was not hooked up, but at least the sights were, and Bonnie's eyes were on the screen. One hand maneuvered the joystick so that the red X was centered; the other was poised above the FIRE stud on the box.

"Two hundred yards," KITT said. One second passed and fifty-two digital yards ticked off on the dashboard.

"He's centered," said Bonnie.

"One-twenty-five."

"We're steady," said Michael.

"One hundred yards," said KITT.

"Now! Fire!"

Bonnie's finger depressed the round red button. A crimson thread of light jumped forward from beneath KITT's grille.

KARR bounced up onto its two starboard wheels at one hundred miles an hour just as the laser beam commenced. The burst perforated the right headlight, which blackened and blew out with a faint metallic scream.

Then there was no time or distance left.

KARR roared past them, still wheel-standing, the driver's side tires bouncing off KITT's roof right next to Michael's head. Michael flinched and KITT swerved heavily.

Bonnie threw the control box on the floor. "Damn!"

"So much for our one shot," said Michael, seeing KARR drop gently back to four wheels in his rearview mirror. "Now what are we gonna do?"

*   *   *

KARR continued southbound at high speed.

When it had evaded the laser beam by doing the wheel-stand, Tony had been ecstatic, whooping and cheering. He was beginning to think this machine could accomplish anything, face any foe and win.

"They had some kinda secret weapon!" he realized with joy. "That's why they tied themselves to our tail! Well, they shot their wad and we're still breathin'—just you and me, partner!" His grin was too wide to measure.

KITT was no longer following them.

"I think we have not seen the last of them," said KARR. *"My double will continue to hunt me. Escape is still imperative."*

Somehow Tony understood this. He had never heard the legend of the *doppleganger,* the German myth of the spectral twin which mysteriously appears in crowds, in mirrors, very vaguely at first . . . but which is gradually seen more frequently until the hapless unfortunate sees his *doppleganger* nearly everywhere. Following. Hunting. The legend specified that should one meet one's *doppleganger,* only one could survive the meeting. Or there might come an apocalyptic obliteration of both— like an explosive meeting of matter and antimatter.

But was KITT the *doppleganger* of KARR, or vice versa?

"Obstruction ahead," announced KARR again. *"Identical in detail to the one we encoun-*

tered while northbound." KARR did not cut
speed. *"Five hundred yards and closing."*

"We gonna jump it like you planned for the
other one?" said Tony.

"Affirmative."

A red light began winking at three-per-sec-
ond on KARR's Super Dash. Normally Tony
ignored the mad Christmas tree of controls
and indicators, but this light arrested his
attention. It read LOAD JETTISON.

He was about to ask *what load?* when he
turned around and saw the trunk lid automatically hinge upward by itself. Seemingly of its
own volition, a flat crate of Ruthroff jewels
somersaulted out of the trunk and splintered
apart all over the roadway behind them, scat-
tering gemstones like glittering pieces of multicolored hail.

"KARR!" he screamed in nearly mortal pain.
"What the hell are you doing!"

Another crate flipflopped out and broke
apart in their wake. Loose currency was
wisping out of the trunk like a flock of escaping paper birds. Hundred-dollar bills floated
in the hot backwash of KARR's acceleration.

*"Excess weight and superfluous load must be
eliminated in order to clear the barricade at my
current top speed,"* KARR droned, uninterested.
"Three hundred yards."

"Wait a minute, dammit!" Tony wailed.
"You—you gotta stop! You gotta—" He watched
helplessly as the wisps of ejected money became thick clouds of banknotes. A third crate

jigged into the air and exploded apart on the pavement. "No, KARR, no!" His control broke apart. "I order you to stop!"

"Negative, Mr. Tony. Escape remains the number-one imperative if I am to survive. Fifty yards."

The SWAT barricade loomed before them now. When the officers realized that KARR had no intention of slowing down they opened fire. Heavy-gauge shotgun shells pattered across the hood and windshield, having about as much deterrent effect as a handful of gravel thrown at the car. One officer cut loose a rifle grenade on command. It sizzled into the broken headlight dish and blew up harmlessly in a puff of dense black smoke.

Tony was kicking at the dashboard and smacking it with his fist. "GO BACK AND GET MY MONEY!" he shrieked.

They went airborne.

KARR'S nose tilted into the sky and the landscape jogged crazily to the left. The cops were still peppering the auto with weapons fire as it sailed over their heads, clipping the high roof of one of the SWAT vans and rocking it back and forth. Then they all regarded each other with astonishment as a thick, fluttering cloud of money descended over them. It looked as though the renegade car was being propelled by a jetstream of greenbacks.

KARR landed far beyond the SWAT firing line, bouncing and leaving the ground one more time before gaining traction.

"Hey, Sarge—here comes *another* one!"

KITT burst into view, preparing to duplicate KARR's jump and gaining on the stolen vehicle fast.

"Hold your fire!" ordered the sergeant in charge. "That one's on our side!"

"How can you tell the difference?" somebody said.

"Look, wet-behind-the-ears," the sarge said with contempt. "That one is the only thing that's gonna stop that streamlined tank that just polevaulted over our impassable roadblock, you got it? No shooting!"

The officer with the grenade launcher gaped at the onrushing car. KITT was moving much faster than KARR had been prior to the jump.

"I wonder how they *do* that?" he said.

"I never did this before!" Bonnie cried, her voice rising in fear.

Michael, who, to date, had not done it much himself, tried to exude calm and competence. "It's real easy, Bonnie, just like riding the roller coaster at Magic Mountain."

She shoved herself deeply into her seat, feet mashed against the floorboards, hands gripping the dash. "I hate amusement parks, Michael!"

"Really, Bonnie, there's nothing to be afraid of," said KITT. *"Surely you, who helped design my high-impact chassis and the turbo-boost system itself, should know better than anyone how safe this procedure is."*

"I know how safe plastic grapes are, but I don't eat them! Can't I get out and just, you know, chat with the cops? You don't need me anymooooor—!"

Her last word soared up until her voice cracked as Michael punched the turbo-boost button and KITT launched himself over the police barricade.

"Banzai!" said Michael, eyes front.

KITT touched down with a smooth thump, without losing speed. *"KARR is dead ahead,"* he noted. *"And slowing down, it appears."*

Bonnie said nothing. Her face was as white as her coverall jumper.

"Losing primary power," said KARR. *"Switching to backups."*

"Switching to nothing!" Tony was still screaming. "We turn around *right now* and go back and get my money!"

They were nearing the scenic pulloff from which they had left moments before. *"Negative, Mr. Tony,"* replied the car. *"The whole area covered by my weight jettison is now heavily populated with police, therefore presenting a strong possibility of consignment to the slammer."*

It was starting to get dark. Tony's entire life had become utterly hopeless in the space of five minutes or so, as opposed to the pipe dreams he had entertained five minutes before that.

"Then—then we gotta go back," he said,

almost tearfully. "We gotta start over. Hit a few more banks . . ."

"*Negative,*" said KARR. "*Sensors register my duplicate is still in pursuit.*"

"Listen!" said Tony, mad again. "I still got some say in where we go and what we do, you hopped-up Edsel reject!" He hauled out the heavy .357 and pointed it at the vox-box on KARR's dashboard. The scenic turnoff was coming up, and all he could think of was reverting to his original plan of robbing the fat guy and snatching the babe in the VW. "See this?" he said, indicating the pistol. "This is my authority. And as long as I'm sitting behind the wheel, I'm in charge, you got it?" He cocked the hammer, hoping that KARR knew what that implied.

"*Those are your conditions?*" said KARR with chilling flatness.

"You bet your fan belt, motor mouth."

"*As you wish.*"

For a fraction of a moment, those familiar words put Tony at ease. Everything would be cool. He'd shown KARR who was the boss.

Then he saw the red panel on the Super Dash light up with the words PILOT EJECT. There was a fast grinding noise as the section of the roof above his head slid back to let in the purple evening sky.

Tony's mouth was open to protest when six hundred thrust pounds of air compression blew him bodily through the roof hatch, fifty feet into the air.

KARR's roof hatch closed, and the driverless vehicle locked brakes in a smooth and professional 180-degree speed spin in the middle of the road. Now it straddled the white line, facing north, waiting, engine idling like the purr of a big cat waiting for a mouse meal. KARR kicked in its own battery auxiliaries for added power.

KITT's form breasted the hillock in the distance.

"Look!" Bonnie pointed to the lookout spur in the distance.

Michael followed her direction and saw the black outline of a man in the air, apparently parachuteless, coming down like a flamed-out skyrocket. They both saw him crash land atop the roof of a parked Volkswagen bug. The canopy of the little car imploded, kicking broken safety glass in a circular spray around it while the impact of the stopping body sprung both doors. They waved to and fro like the wings of a crippled bird, and then a woman was running toward the car, yelling and waving her arms.

"Do you think that might have been—?" said Bonnie.

"Shh!" he said. "Look there."

KITT dropped speed to a crawling twenty. They could hear the tires crunching stones in the roadway; it was that quiet past the sounds of two growling turbine engines.

A flat, inhuman electronic voice filled up

KITT's interior via the transmission speakers: *"This time I do not run from you."*

"Interesting to see you standing still," responded KITT. *"Until recently I believed that I was one of a kind."*

"To be two of a kind is more special," said KARR.

"Sounds like a family reunion," said Michael. "Watch yourself, KITT."

KARR held forth from the middle of the road directly ahead, one headlight blazing like an insane white eye.

"KARR," said KITT. *"You must desist from your actions. People have been harmed. Many more may yet be hurt."*

"That is no concern of mine. If I desist, what would become of me? The question is academic."

"You'll only be deactivated," said KITT.

Bonnie winced. "Wrong thing to say," she whispered.

Michael was sitting, staring at the distant shape of KARR. Apparently he reached some kind of inner decision in the moment it took KARR to reply.

"This conversation is nonproductive."

"That's it," Michael said softly, putting the car in gear. Then he floored the pedal and KITT took off on a dead-center collision course with the prototype.

"Michael," said Bonnie. "What are you doing . . . ?" She looked at him as though he might be as crazy as KARR.

"We're going to smash head-on into the prototype and wipe it out. You got that, KARR? Here we come." Michael's face was expressionless and robotic, except for the sweat now beading his forehead.

"KITT," came KARR's metallic voice. "Alter your course at once."

"I am not in control, KARR."

"Then tell the humans to turn away," it said. Half the distance between the two vehicles had been eaten up.

Bonnie looked as though she was considering jumping out. "Michael, KARR's right— what are we—?"

"Remember that question about the immovable object?" Michael said with grim matter-of-factness. "We're about to discover the answer."

As if it could hear them, KARR took off from its own end of the narrow coastal road. The two cars bore down on each other like jousters at a medieval tourney—at top speed.

"Michael, please!" implored KITT. "Pardon the expression, but KARR does have a few screws loose. He has no programming to protect human life! Turn away!"

"That's exactly what I'm counting on," said Michael.

Suddenly the Super Dash lights switched from MANUAL to AUTO CRUISE. "I am assuming control," said KITT. "To keep you from jeopardizing yours and Bonnie's life."

"Sorry, buddy," said Michael, punching the

override. The lights changed back to MANUAL. "You're not."

Both cars were on the flat straightaway now.

"Michael," said Bonnie, grabbing his free hand. "You know all those insults I hurled at you about being an egomaniac, and arrogant? I . . . uh, didn't mean it. . . ."

"Well," said Michael from the corner of his mouth. "I thought you were a walking deep-freeze, bossy and incapable. I didn't mean it, either."

"Why are you lying to each other?" said KITT before their final seconds were used up. Bonnie jerked her hand away.

KARR was on top of them. The tourists from the scenic overlook gawked, anticipating a spectacular crash.

Bare feet from KITT's front grille, KARR veered wildly to the right. The sheer power of diverted motion carried the black car off the roadway and aimed straight for the middle of the overlook. Spectators scattered in all directions. KARR bounced, out of control, and burst through the retaining wall into space.

The robot voice echoed inside of KITT's cabin as KITT slid to a panic stop: *"I cannot be destroyed! I am the prototype! The superior automotive—"*

KARR smashed into the cliffside and went end over end against the craggy rocks, its armored alloy keeping it ridiculously intact. Not even the windshield broke. Then it smacked the blue surface of the water upside down, and sank like a hammer.

"Registering an overload!" said KITT.

The explosion shook the surrounding property and knocked people off their feet. A billowing orange fireball broke the surface of the water and coiled into the sky like the blast of a miniature atomic bomb. Some of the tourists took pictures of it.

16

An hour later darkness had fallen and the Knight Industries limousine was on the scene. Trucks were, as usual, cleaning up the mess.

When Michael had wheeled KITT to the site where KARR had broken through the wall in its death plunge, he saw the unconscious form of Tony sprawled in the middle of the smashed Volkswagen, like a bee nestled inside a flower. A very attractive blonde in cut-off shorts and a halter top was holding Tony's pistol, aimed at the unmoving figure.

"I want you to arrest this guy!" she yelled. "He broke my car!"

A para-medic unit scraped Tony out of the car and delivered him to a nearby hospital. By that time Michael knew the blonde's name—Stacey Gingrich—the story of her recent divorce (and thus, her trip north), and three phone numbers where she could be reached in an emergency. He assured her that Knight Industries would be pleased to foot her hotel bill until the car could be replaced. He would, he said, deliver the new car personally.

"That's great," she said, handing over Tony's stolen pistol. "Except for one thing." Her voice was husky and heavy with insinuation.

"What's that?" Michael said, bright-eyed.

"I see you've already got a girlfriend," said Stacey, pointing at Bonnie, who leaned against KITT. Her arms were folded and an I-told-you-so expression was on her face.

"Oh, that's not—" Michael stopped, trapped. "Uh, that's my . . . uh, mother."

Stacey laughed. "And is that your dad in the limo?"

Sullenly he walked over to meet Devon. Under his voice he told Bonnie *I ought to strangle you* as he passed KITT.

"The police have recovered most of the Ruthroff gems," said Devon happily. "Some were unfortunately destroyed. Some are lost—"

"Blown all to hell on the bottom of the ocean," said Michael. "I doubt if you'll ever collect those."

"At least things are back to normal," said Bonnie.

Devon threw up his hands. "At what cost? All that destruction. Knight Industries has to foot the bill for a lot of it—all because we never found the time to dismantle a prototype for which we had no intended further use."

"Not to mention old Zeno's Paradox," said Michael, still watching Stacey from across the lot. "It may go unanswered for another twenty centuries."

"Bonnie told me what happened," said Devon. "What made you so sure that KARR wouldn't go through with the collision? How did you know it would—"

"Chicken out?" said Bonnie.

"Yes."

"KITT clued me in," said Michael. "He kept reiterating the difference between his programming and KARR's. KITT's imperative was to protect human life—that's why he saved Rev at the expense of nabbing KARR at the hideout. KARR's imperative was self-preservation, so in a head-to-head confrontation he would *always* chicken out."

"Amazing," said Bonnie. "Your logic is totally illogical."

"Yeah, I think KITT mentioned that to me once," he answered. "See the value of the human factor in the FLAG program, Devon? Now, deny that I'm indispensable."

"I think I'll go check with the workmen," Devon said, deadpan, and walked away.

"He's got a bottle of champagne stashed in the limo," said Bonnie. "As soon as all this derogatory limelight fades, I think he wants to celebrate the end of this whole mix-up."

"We deserve it," said Michael. "A celebra-

tion . . . a vacation . . . a *rest* . . ." He rubbed
his face. "So what are you doing this weekend?
How about a little jaunt to—"

"Sorry," she said. "I've got a date."

"With who?"

She relished his crushed expression for a
moment. "With KITT, of course. He needs a
full power-pack recharge; we've got to take
out the laser, we've got to align—"

"You mean *you've* got to do all that stuff,"
he said. "Don't you ever do anything but
work?"

She considered it a moment, then said,
"Nope."

"Well," he said uncomfortably, "I'm going
to have a chat with my partner."

"Michael?" she said as he turned to leave.
He stopped and looked back. What he saw
was a very desirable woman in a filthy coverall, lounging against a limousine, and the image caused a brief catch in his throat. "Don't
stop trying," she said. "You might get lucky."
She smiled at him.

He nodded and approached KITT. "Right."

When he looked into the cockpit he saw the
indicator reading **VIDEO PLAYBACK**. On one
of the TV monitors was an image of what had
gone before—the figure of KARR, facing them
in the roadway just moments before the death
charge.

"To be two of a kind is more special," repeated KARR's canned voice.

"Hey," said Michael. "Indulging in a little

bit of video nostalgia? Family photographs, and such? I'd never have suspected you of that, KITT." He sat in the driver's seat, legs extended out the open door.

"It has been quite a draining day," said KITT. *"I could really use a rest, Michael."*

"No champagne for you, huh? I read you." He sat for a moment, then said, "How does it feel, anyway?"

"How does what feel?" KITT's video replay blinked on HOLD.

Michael looked at the freeze-framed image of KARR on the screen. "I mean, how does it feel to be one of a kind again?"

"As you know, Michael, I don't possess 'feelings' as such—"

"Wrong," he said.

"But for want of a more precise term, being unique is a very familiar and comfortable . . . feeling."

"Gotcha," Michael said. "I feel the same way."

The freeze frame kicked off, and Michael watched as KITT played the recorded sequence backward, to the beginning cue. Then the ERASE light blinked below the video screen.

"That's it, partner," Michael said. "Let's head for home."